WHEN LOVE DIE

Steven felt himself stiffen. "It's none of my business what Tricia does. We're not going together anymore."

"Then what are you getting so excited about?" Cara asked.

"I'm not excited!" Steven practically roared. Abruptly he pulled Cara to her feet. "Let's dance. I feel like dancing." *To hell with Tricia*, he thought.

Steven placed his arms around Cara. He closed his eyes, imagining it was Tricia he was holding. Tricia's warm body pressed so closely to his, Tricia's fingertips dancing lightly over the back of his neck—

Suddenly Steven kissed Cara hard on the lips.

Cara stirred eagerly in his arms. "Oh, Steve," she murmured. "This is going to be the nicest party I ever had."

Bantam Books in the Sweet Valley High Series
Ask your bookseller for the books you have missed

#1 DOUBLE LOVE
#2 SECRETS
#3 PLAYING WITH FIRE
#4 POWER PLAY
#5 ALL NIGHT LONG
#6 DANGEROUS LOVE
#7 DEAR SISTER
#8 HEARTBREAKER
#9 RACING HEARTS
#10 WRONG KIND OF GIRL
#11 TOO GOOD TO BE TRUE
#12 WHEN LOVE DIES
#13 KIDNAPPED!
#14 DECEPTIONS

SWEET VALLEY HIGH

WHEN LOVE DIES

Written by
Kate William

Created by
FRANCINE PASCAL

BANTAM BOOKS
TORONTO · NEW YORK · LONDON · SYDNEY · AUCKLAND

RL 6, IL age 12 and up

WHEN LOVE DIES
A Bantam Book / September 1984

Sweet Valley High is a trademark of Francine Pascal

Conceived by Francine Pascal

Produced by Cloverdale Press Inc.,
133 Fifth Avenue, New York, N.Y. 10003

Cover art by James Mathewuse

ISBN 0-553-24358-6

Published simultaneously in the United States and Canada

Bantam Books are published by Bantam Books, Inc. Its trademark,
consisting of the words "Bantam Books" and the portrayal of a rooster,
is Registered in U.S. Patent and Trademark Office and in other
countries. Marca Registrada. Bantam Books, Inc., 666 Fifth Avenue,
New York, New York 10103.

PRINTED IN THE UNITED STATES OF AMERICA

O   0 9 8 7 6 5 4 3 2

To Amy Berkower

One

"Steve! Aren't you going to say hi to your favorite sister?"

Jessica Wakefield tossed her schoolbooks down on the kitchen counter in an untidy pile. Her wide, aquamarine eyes flashed with curiosity as she took in her older brother's miserable expression. Steven was sitting slumped at the table, staring vacantly into space while he stirred a cup of coffee that had probably gone cold hours ago.

He looked up and blinked, as if seeing her for the first time. "Hi, uh . . . Jess," he said, as if it had taken him a second or two to tell which of his twin sisters was standing before him.

1

Boy, what's wrong with him? Jessica wondered. *He can't even tell who's who.*

On the outside, there was no denying that Jessica and Elizabeth were identical in every respect. They shared the same sun-streaked golden hair and dazzling white smiles, the same delicate features and perfect size-six figures. Together, they formed a double image of sun-kissed, all-American loveliness.

Beneath the surface, however, it was a different matter. Tempestuous Jessica seemed to attract trouble the way a magnet draws metal shavings, while the more levelheaded Elizabeth spent a lot of her time trying to disengage herself from the results of her sister's mischief-making. But at the moment Jessica was honestly concerned about her brother. She sank down in the chair beside his.

"What's wrong? You look like your best friend just died."

Steven grunted. "It's nothing." He stopped stirring his coffee and put the spoon aside. His brown eyes were dark with gloom; his wavy brown hair looked as if it hadn't been combed. The shadow of a two-day beard darkened his handsome, square-cut face.

"Nothing! You've been walking around here every weekend looking like Dracula's leftovers. You're still upset about Tricia, right? More upset than *she* is, I'll bet."

It really bugged her the way her brother car-

2

ried on about the trouble he was having with his dumb girlfriend—as if she were really, well, *somebody*. In Jessica's opinion Tricia Martin was a nobody. No, worse than a nobody. Tricia came from one of the trashiest families in Sweet Valley. What on earth did Steven see in her anyway? Jessica wondered. She snatched a banana from the fruit bowl, and angrily yanked the peel off.

"Look, Jess, just lay off, OK?" Steven shot her a warning glare as he got up and stalked out of the room. Jessica saw that there were tears in his eyes.

A few moments later Elizabeth sailed into the kitchen, put down an armful of books, and removed her sweater. "Hi, Jess," she said, heading straight for the refrigerator. "Gosh, I'm starved! I'm going to make myself a sandwich. You hungry?"

"Not really," Jessica said as she popped the rest of the banana into her mouth, leaving the peel on the table. She watched as Elizabeth took a big piece of cheese out of the refrigerator and placed it on the counter.

The two girls could have been mirror images, except that Jessica's hair swung loose around her shoulders while Elizabeth's was pulled back in a practical ponytail. And Elizabeth's neatly tailored corduroy skirt was a lot less likely to bring traffic to a screeching halt than Jessica's skintight jeans and flimsy camisole top.

3

"Liz, did you see Steve on your way in?" Jessica demanded as her sister spread mustard on a slice of bread. "He looks awful," she went on, without waiting for an answer. "I wonder if Tricia finally dumped him."

Jessica thrived on real-life soap operas—especially those in which she played a starring role. However, a crisis involving their adored older brother came in a close second.

"I always said Steve was too good for her, didn't I?" she continued. "I always said she'd turn out to be nothing but trouble—just like that whole grungy family of hers. I guess this just proves I'm right."

Elizabeth turned to give her sister a sharp look. "Our poor brother is dragging around with a broken heart, and all you can think about is being right. Don't you care about Steve?"

"Of course I do!" Jessica flared. "I *was* thinking of Steve. If he'd listened to me, he never would have gotten so involved with Tricia in the first place. He should have broken off with her months ago."

"I think you've got things mixed up," Elizabeth said sternly. "Steve doesn't *want* to break up with her. He's madly in love with Tricia."

"Ugh! How could he be? Talk about humiliating! The Martins are just about the worst family in Sweet Valley. How could our own brother want to be *seen* with one of them?" Jessica

4

jumped up to face Elizabeth across the kitchen counter.

"Tricia's nice," Elizabeth protested, meeting her sister's gaze. "She's not like the rest of her family."

"If she's so nice, why's she giving Steve the cold shoulder?" Jessica walked over to the counter and snatched a piece of the cheese Elizabeth had been slicing.

Elizabeth sighed. There was no denying Tricia had been acting coldly toward Steve, Elizabeth thought. She'd broken two dates, and according to Steven, she'd acted vague and uninterested when they were together. It was strange because Tricia had always been so devoted to him in the past.

"I don't know what's going on with Tricia," Elizabeth said. "Maybe she's having some kind of trouble at home. Something she's too embarrassed to tell Steve."

"I can't see what could be more embarrassing than what he already knows. I mean, everybody knows her father's a drunk, for goodness' sake. And her sister! Betsy'll probably end up either pregnant or in jail in another year or so. Maybe both."

"Come on, Jess, give Tricia a break. Her family's problems aren't her fault."

"Why does she have to go around defending them all the time then? Honestly, she's so forgiving it makes me want to throw up!"

"I don't suppose you've ever heard of family loyalty?" Elizabeth asked pointedly.

Jessica sniffed. "All I know is I could use a little of it myself. It seems like every time I try to do somebody a favor around here, I practically get my head bitten off. Last week I merely *suggested* to Steve that Tricia might be interested in another guy, and he looked at me like I'd just thrown a hand grenade at him."

"Some favor," Elizabeth muttered. She put her sandwich on a plate and carried it over to the table.

Jessica tagged after her, sitting down in the chair next to her. "OK, so what's the latest? Do you know why Steve looks so lousy? What gives?"

Elizabeth took a big bite of her sandwich. "He didn't tell me. But I heard him on the phone asking for Tricia when I walked in. I guess she wasn't home, because he hung up."

"She stood him up, I'll bet. She'd probably rather be off at some wild party than spending time with someone whose biggest interest is college. She's just like Betsy."

"What's Betsy got to do with it?" As far as Elizabeth could see, Tricia wasn't anything like her older sister, who had one of the worst reputations in town.

"Well, you know how it is, they're sisters—and sisters have lots of things in common," Jessica finished lamely.

6

Elizabeth laughed. "For my sake, I hope that's not true—or I'm in real trouble!"

"See what I mean?" Jessica sulked. "Nobody around here appreciates me. Someday when I'm rich and famous, you'll be sorry you weren't nicer."

Elizabeth laughed. "We love you, dummy—isn't that enough? Anyway, to show you how much I appreciate you, here—you can have the rest of my sandwich."

Jessica glared at the crust on Elizabeth's plate. "Gee, thanks a lot. I'm overwhelmed by your generosity."

"What did you expect? A check for a million dollars?"

Jessica looked thoughtful. "That wouldn't be bad—for starters. Actually, I was thinking maybe you could lend me your red shoes for tonight. I'm going out with Aaron Dallas and—"

Elizabeth didn't let her finish. "Absolutely, positively *no*. The last time you borrowed them, you broke a strap, and it cost me six dollars to get it fixed. You never did pay me back."

"I haven't forgotten. I was planning to pay you back. Every cent. Didn't I promise?"

"Yeah, six months ago."

"OK, so this time I promise I'll pay you back with interest. Now can I borrow them?"

Elizabeth refused to budge. "Sorry, Jess."

"In that case, I guess I'll just have to go barefoot. I'll probably end up stepping on a piece of broken glass and bleeding to death, and it'll be all your fault." Jessica rose from her chair with a wounded expression. "If you can live with that on your conscience . . ."

Elizabeth burst into uncontrollable giggles. "I give. A performance like that deserves some reward. Honestly, Jess, Hollywood just doesn't know what it's missing. You could probably win an Academy Award."

"And when I do, I'll be sure to thank my sweet, generous sister for having the same size feet as me." Jessica laughed and leaned over to give her twin a playful punch on the arm.

Later that evening, Elizabeth was getting ready for her date with Todd Wilkins, her boyfriend and the handsome star of the Sweet Valley High basketball team. She imagined his warm brown eyes, his lopsided grin. She smiled as she slipped a navy T-shirt dress over her head. After all this time, the thought of Todd still made her tingle. She barely noticed when Jessica waltzed into her room and began digging around in her closet, looking for the red shoes.

"Steve hardly said two words at dinner. This thing with Tricia is really getting out of hand. Somebody should do something."

Elizabeth shot her sister a warning look. "Keep out of it, Jess. If Steve wants our advice, he'll ask for it."

As if on cue, their older brother walked in

through the open door. "Has either of you seen my car keys?"

At six feet plus, Steven towered over his sisters, but aside from the healthy outdoor look they all shared, he didn't resemble them in the least. With his rangy, athletic build, wavy, brown hair, and dark eyes he was an eighteen-year-old version of their father.

"Got a date, Steve?" Jessica piped up.

"I thought I'd drive over and see Tricia. She wasn't home when I called, but she should be back by now."

"Didn't you tell her you were coming home for the weekend?" Jessica asked.

Steven frowned. "She knows I come home almost every weekend. I've never had to make a big thing of telling her."

"Oh, I see." Jessica picked up Elizabeth's brush and began guiding it through her hair with studied casualness. "Maybe you're giving her the impression that you can take her for granted. You know, you just expect her to be there for you."

"It's not like that with Trish and me," Steven protested. "We love each other."

"Well, you *did* say she's been acting sort of standoffish lately."

Elizabeth jumped in to the rescue. "Maybe she's distracted by something at home," she suggested, shooting her sister a pointed look.

Jessica yawned. "So what's new about that?"

9

Wearing a worried expression, Steven slumped down on the bed. "If something is wrong, she won't tell me what it is." He stared down at his hands in helpless frustration. "I'd give anything to know why she's been acting this way."

"Maybe she's the one who's taking you for granted," Jessica said, deftly changing tack. "She knows she's got you, so why bother working at it?"

"Tricia's not like that. You don't know her like I do."

"If you know her so well, then I don't see what the problem is. I thought people who were that close could talk to each other about anything."

Obviously Steven had thought so, too. The possibility that he might have misjudged the depth of Tricia's love was more than a little disturbing.

"I guess she'll tell me what's wrong when she's ready," he said, not sounding too hopeful.

Jessica's eyes narrowed. "Maybe it's not a *what*," she suggested slyly. "Maybe it's a *who*."

Steven glowered at her. "Look, Jess, if you're going to start that business about Tricia sneaking around behind my back with some other guy, I don't want to hear it. She wouldn't do anything like that."

Jessica flashed him a knowing smile. "Whatever you say, big brother."

"If there were some other guy, I'd know it,

wouldn't I? People would have seen them around together."

"Of course, you're probably right," Jessica agreed.

"It's a small town. You couldn't hide something like that forever."

"But, Steve," she said sweetly, "I thought you said Tricia wasn't the type?"

Steven flushed a dark red. Elizabeth glared at her sister, then went over and put her arm around Steven's shoulders. She couldn't bear seeing her brother in so much misery.

"It's silly to jump to conclusions," Elizabeth said. "And I agree with you, Steve. Tricia's not the type to fool around behind your back. Besides, why would she even want someone else? You're the one she loves."

Steven's frown deepened. "I always thought that, too. But right now I'm not so sure. Something's changed. I don't know what, but I'm going to find out." He stood up, his jaw set at a determined angle. "Tonight."

Two

It was only a few miles from the Wakefields'
comfortable split-level ranch house in a beautiful
green area of Sweet Valley to the poorer section
of town where the Martins lived, but as far
as Steven was concerned, it was a completely
different world. His headlights picked up the
gleam of discarded cans and broken glass that
littered the weeds alongside the uneven road.
He pulled to a stop in front of a shabby frame
house with peeling paint. *Tricia's house.* As
always, he experienced a pang at the thought.
Sweet, lovely Tricia deserved much better than
this, though he had never once heard her
complain about it.

Steven's chest was heavy with apprehension as he waited by the front door for his knock to be answered. Would she be home? Would she want to see him? When he had called, her father had said he didn't know where she was or when she would be back. Strange. Tricia knew he was coming home for the weekend. He always called her Friday afternoon when he got in—and she always answered the phone on the first or second ring, her voice slightly breathless, as if she'd had to run to catch it. Then she gave that happy, eager laugh when she heard him say hello. At least that was the way it used to be. Lately . . .

The door shrieked open on rusted hinges. A man stood swaying in the blue-gray light that flickered from an old TV set. He wore a stained undershirt tucked into baggy old pants, and he smelled strongly of liquor. Steven cringed, even while he arranged his face into a friendly smile.

"Hi, Mr. Martin. Is Tricia home?"

Tricia's father blinked, as if trying to bring Steven into focus. "Yuh, she's here," he slurred, "but she can't see you. She's busy. Sorry, Steve."

Steven felt as if he'd been kicked in the stomach. "Where is she?" he asked. "I have to talk to her."

"She's in her room, but she said if you came by to tell you—"

Steven didn't wait to hear the rest. Angrily, he brushed past Mr. Martin, heading straight for Tricia's room. The door was closed, but he didn't bother to knock. Tricia looked up with wide, startled eyes as he strode in.

At the sight of her, Steven's heart caught, and the anger drained out of him. She was so beautiful, with her delicate features, creamy skin, and strawberry-blond hair. She reminded him of a porcelain doll. Yet there was nothing doll-like about the way her brilliant blue eyes leaped with fire or the quick, light grace of her movements.

"Steve." One slender hand fluttered to her throat, but she revealed no other sign of emotion. "I—I was going to call and let you know. . . ." She sneaked a guilty glance at the suitcase that lay open on her bed. "I'm going to be out of town for the weekend."

With a hot rush, Steven's heart started up again. "This is kind of sudden, isn't it?"

"I'm sorry, Steve." She spoke so softly he had to strain to catch her words. "It's just that— well, something came up. I am really sorry. I know I should have let you know sooner than this."

He glared at the half-packed suitcase. "Where are you going?"

"I told you. Out of town."

"That could be anywhere. Come on, Trish. It's me you're talking to. Steve. Remember? The guy you're supposed to be in love with. What in God's name is going on here? You've been

14

avoiding me for weeks, and now *this*." He gestured angrily toward the suitcase. "I can hardly believe any of this is happening. It's like being in a bad dream."

Two bright spots of color formed on her pale cheeks. "I guess this is it then," she said wearily.

"This is what?" Steven responded in confusion.

"You want to break up. Don't worry, Steve. I understand. I'm—I'm sure it's better this way."

"Wait a minute! What are you talking about? I never said I wanted to break up. I love you, Trish. All I want are some answers." He gripped her by the shoulders. "Trish, can't you tell me what's going on?" he asked gently. "I *know* there's something wrong. Why can't you trust me enough to tell me?"

Her head dropped forward, her hair sliding down to shield her expression. "There's nothing wrong, Steve," she replied woodenly. "It's just—well, lately I've been thinking maybe we shouldn't see so much of each other. Look, you're away at college most of the time. I'm sure there are plenty of girls you could go out with."

"You're the only one I want!" he protested brokenly, tears filling his eyes. "Unless . . ."

Tricia's head snapped back. A strange emotion blazed in her eyes. "Unless what?"

"Trish, are you trying to tell me you're tired of me? That you want to go out with other guys?" Steven didn't realize how tightly he was gripping her until she winced.

She didn't answer. She just stood there, looking at him in that strange way, her eyes burning into him. The force of her silence was like a blow. Suddenly Steven knew it was true, the thing he'd been avoiding all this time.

He felt himself growing tight and angry once again. "You've met someone else, haven't you? You're going away with him for the weekend. That's what you don't want to tell me, isn't it?"

Tricia stood pale and still, except for the slight trembling that shook her from head to foot. She didn't say a word.

Steve stared at her in disbelief. Finally he said, "I trusted you. I loved you. I thought you loved me. God, Tricia, do you have any idea how I feel right now? It's like part of me is dying."

"It's better this way, Steve." She spoke mechanically.

"Yeah, I'll bet it is. For you." Abruptly he released her and turned away angrily. He had to get out. He felt as if someone had jabbed him in the gut.

"One more thing," he said in a bitter voice. "Whoever he is, wish him luck for me. I hope he makes out better than I did."

Tricia winced as if he'd struck him, but she made no move to stop him. It was only after she heard the thud of the front door slamming

16

shut that a single word escaped her like a sigh, half whispered, half moaned: "Steve . . ."

She collapsed onto the bed like a dress slipping from its hanger. She felt so cold, yet when she brought her hands to her cheeks, her face was burning. Scalding tears spilled down her cheeks. Except for the bare bulb casting a fierce white circle of light on the ceiling, the room seemed full of shadows, all crowding in on her.

Her fists were clenched so tightly that she could feel her fingernails digging into her palms. *I can't tell him. It's better if he doesn't know the truth. Let him think I betrayed him. It's better if he hates me.*

But the feeling that she was doing the right thing did nothing to lessen her misery. With a strangled cry, Tricia turned her face into the pillow. All the emotion she'd held back for Steven's sake came rushing forth in heaving sobs that felt as if they were being torn from her insides, leaving emptiness in their place.

She hadn't known it would be so painful losing Steven. Hurting him the way she had was almost more than she could bear. It was all she could do to keep from breaking down and admitting the truth. But the truth would only hurt him more, she reminded herself sorrowfully.

Tricia could still hear the doctor's words echoing in her mind. ". . . *We'll do everything we can, but. . . . With treatment, perhaps six months. . . .*"

She hadn't believed it then, but she had fi-

17

nally begun to accept it. Leukemia. Such an ugly, awful-sounding word. It had haunted her most of her life—ever since her mother had died of it. Tricia had been nine at the time, but she could still remember those dark, horrible days, the dim bedroom smelling of medicine, her mother's gaunt face against the pillow. Her mother had always been so cheerful and full of smiles, but in the end she had wasted away to a dull-eyed skeleton. When she died, it was as if a light had gone out of their lives, especially her husband's. He couldn't seem to pull himself together. Drinking was the only thing that numbed the pain. He had loved his wife so much that something in him died with her. He couldn't face the awful loneliness of life without her.

Tricia didn't want that to happen to Steven. Better to have him stop loving her. Better to have him think she was going away for the weekend with someone else. If he knew the truth—that she was going to the hospital for treatment—he would be devastated. He would only hang on more tightly.

This way it wouldn't hurt so much. Knowing she'd lost him was nearly as terrible as knowing she was going to die. But when you loved someone, you had to sacrifice your own feelings for theirs. This was her sacrifice. Her gift to Steven. The last gift she would ever be able to give him.

Three

Cara Walker slid into the seat next to Jessica's just as the bus started up. Outside, the white-columned facade of Sweet Valley High, with its Romanesque clock and sprawl of green lawn, swept slowly past.

"Is it true?" Cara asked, her brown eyes shining hopefully. She flipped her smooth, dark hair over one tanned shoulder as she leaned closer to her best friend.

Jessica looked up from the magazine she was reading. "Is what true?"

"*You* know," Cara replied impatiently. "About Steve and Tricia. Did they really break up?"

"Oh, that. Yeah, it's true. And it's about time Steve dumped her, too."

"Steve dumped *her*?"

"Naturally," Jessica answered in annoyance. "You didn't think any brother of mine would get dumped by a *Martin*, for goodness' sake."

"No—no, of course not." Cara leaned even closer in her eagerness not to miss a single juicy word. "How did it happen? I want you to tell me everything."

Jessica smiled. Besides being her best friend, Cara was one of the biggest gossips in school. Anything she told Cara was sure to be spread over the entire campus by the next day. This was Jessica's chance to make sure Steven didn't change his mind and go back to that creepy Tricia. Besides, she knew Cara had a personal interest in Steven. She'd always had sort of a crush on him. Maybe that would come in handy, too.

"I don't know all the details," Jessica said in a hushed voice. "All I know is that Tricia's definitely *out*. Steve told me so himself. Good riddance is what I say. Now maybe Steve can find himself a girlfriend from a decent family for a change."

Cara pretended a sudden exaggerated interest in a piece of fluff that was sticking up from a rip in the seat. "Any candidates so far?"

"Not yet, but I'm sure it won't be long. After all, Steve's not too bad-looking."

Cara's head snapped up. "Are you kidding? Your brother is a genuine, certified *hunk*. I wish—" She bit her lip.

"You wish what?" Jessica's aquamarine eyes took on a mischievous gleam.

Cara was blushing furiously. "Never mind. It was nothing."

"Oh, come on, Cara, why don't you just admit it?"

"Admit what?"

"That you're dying to go out with my brother."

"I never said I was dying to go out with Steve," she replied defensively.

Jessica giggled. "No, if you don't count the first thousand times. But even if you hadn't, silly, it's written all over your face."

Instinctively Cara's hands flew to her cheeks. "Oh, Jess, is it that obvious? Do you think Steve knows?"

"Don't worry about Steve. Right now he wouldn't know a brick wall if he ran into it."

Cara sighed. "Great. Does that mean I'll have to hit him over the head to get him to notice me?"

"I've got an even better idea. Don't forget— you have a secret weapon."

"What secret weapon?"

"Me!" Jessica's smile widened to a dazzling grin. "With me on your side, Steve doesn't stand a chance."

Cara sat back, dazed with happiness. "Wow!

I can hardly believe it. Finally. Imagine me going to all those neat college parties with your fabulous brother. . . ."

Jessica made a face. "Somehow I can't picture Steve as fabulous. Sweet and lovable, yes. Fabulous, no."

"That's just because he's your brother. I don't think my brother is very cute either."

"Your brother's only thirteen. Nobody's cute at that age."

As the bus stopped at a red light, Cara said, "Gosh, I almost forgot to tell you. Did you hear what happened to Jeremy Frank?"

"You mean *the* Jeremy Frank?"

"The one and only."

Everyone in Sweet Valley who owned a television set knew who Jeremy Frank was. He was the host of a popular local talk show called "Frankly Speaking." He also happened to be tall, dark, and gorgeous, with the bluest eyes to hit the screen since Paul Newman. Practically every girl in Sweet Valley had a crush on him. Jessica was one of the lucky few who had actually seen him. She'd spotted him coming out of a supermarket once and had nearly dropped her bag of groceries. He was even cuter in person.

Cara sighed. "It's so tragic."

"Don't tell me he got married!" Jessica cried in panic. She could think of no worse tragedy.

"Gosh no. Nothing as bad as that."

"Whew," Jessica breathed. "You had me worried for a minute. What did happen?"

"He broke his leg. He's in the hospital."

"Oh, no! That's awful. How did it happen?"

"He ran into a tree when he was skiing. I heard all about it from Janie McBride. She's a candy striper at Fowler Memorial. She even got him to autograph his picture. Boy, I'd give anything to trade places with her. What luck!"

"Just remember," Jessica was quick to remind Cara, "you're not supposed to be thinking about other men. You're saving yourself for Steve." *But I'm free to do as I please*, she added silently, conjuring up an image of Jeremy Frank's handsome face. Cara had given her a great idea.

"How can I be saving myself for someone who doesn't even know I exist?" Cara wailed.

"He will, he will. Just leave it to me," Jessica assured her friend, although her thoughts were elsewhere.

Now confident of Jessica's help in her efforts to interest Steven, Cara moved on to the next item of gossip. She was like a fountain of information on the latest happenings in Sweet Valley— a fountain that never ran dry.

"I heard something interesting at lunch today," she said. "Lila told me there's a new family moving into the Godfrey mansion. According to her, they're *fabulously* rich. And they've got an eighteen-year-old son she says is a real hunk. I wonder what kind of car he drives?"

Jessica stopped daydreaming about Jeremy and started concentrating on what Cara was saying. "What's their name?" she asked.

"Something with an M—Morrow, I think."

Jessica had heard her father mention that name. Probably because Ned Wakefield had been Morgan Godfrey's lawyer until Mr. Godfrey's death a few years back, and he still handled his estate. Jessica had been to the mansion only once, but it had made a lasting impression on her. It was by far the most fabulous house in Sweet Valley, even grander than the Fowlers' mansion. Actually, it was more like a palace than a mansion, complete with marble arches, an indoor swimming pool, and servants' quarters. The thought of a new family moving in was an exciting one. Jessica made a mental note to pump her father for more information when she saw him.

Cara jumped up as the bus halted at her stop. "Got to go. Call me later, OK? I can't wait to hear what kind of plan you're cooking up for Steve and me."

Two stops later, Jessica got off the bus and raced home, her mind busily clicking away. The get-Cara-and-Steven-together scheme could wait. She had something more important on her mind, but she'd need Elizabeth's help.

She found her sister upstairs in her bedroom.

24

Elizabeth always got back from school earlier on the days when Todd gave her a ride. Jessica flopped down on her twin's bed, scattering the articles Elizabeth had been proofreading for *The Oracle*, the school paper.

Jessica gave a huge sigh and announced, "Life has no meaning."

Elizabeth greeted this statement with only the tiniest flicker of surprise. After sixteen years, she was used to her twin's theatrics.

"Jess, what are you talking about?" she asked.

Jessica rolled onto her stomach, propping her chin with her elbows. "To be more to the point, *our* lives have no meaning. Have you ever thought about it, Liz? I mean *really* thought about how boring and meaningless our lives are?"

"I guess I haven't," Elizabeth replied, a note of amusement in her voice. "How could my life be boring with you around?"

Jessica plowed ahead as if she hadn't heard Elizabeth's comment. "Our lives are so narrow," she intoned dramatically. "Besides going to school, we never *do* anything. Nothing important and worthwhile."

Elizabeth smiled. "You mean Jessica Wakefield thinks there's something more worthwhile than broad shoulders and blue eyes?"

Jessica let out another deep sigh and rolled her eyes. "Honestly, Liz, I don't see how you can joke about it. I'm completely serious."

Elizabeth darted her sister a knowing look as she gathered the articles into a pile. "OK, Jess, who is he this time?"

She'd been through this song and dance with Jessica more times than she could count. There was always some boy Jessica swore she couldn't live without. Without him life had no meaning—even while half a dozen other guys were practically beating her door down to get a date with her.

"How can you be so crass?" Jessica demanded indignantly. "This has nothing to do with a boy. What I'm talking about is giving up a few hours a week to bring comfort to the sick."

"Huh?" Elizabeth stared at her sister as if she'd just announced she were going to run for president.

"Liz, I think we should volunteer to be candy stripers over at the hospital."

"Jess, have you gone nuts?"

"What's so crazy about it?"

"Nothing. It's just that I never expected you to be so, uh—interested in sick people."

"How can you say that? Don't you remember the last time we watched *Love Story* on TV? I used up an entire box of tissues, and that was only for the first half."

Elizabeth sighed. "I don't think I'll ever forget."

For weeks afterward, Jessica had pretended to feel faint whenever a boy she liked came

26

near, in hopes he'd think she had some romantic, incurable disease. It ended the day she pulled her act on Tom McKay and he'd commented nervously that he hoped whatever she had wasn't catching.

"Well?" Jessica demanded. "What about it?"

"I don't know," Elizabeth said. "I'm awfully busy as it is with the paper and everything."

"But this is our big chance to save lives! Think of it! How can you turn your back on all those poor patients?"

"I never heard of a candy striper saving anyone's life," Elizabeth remarked dryly. "From what I hear, all they do is go around passing out magazines and making sure no one dies of thirst. Besides, you don't need me to join. If you want to be a candy striper so badly, why don't you volunteer on your own?"

"Oh, please, Liz! It just wouldn't be the same without you. We've always done everything together. Anyway, Dad trusts you to drive the Fiat more than he trusts me."

"I think I'm beginning to get the picture."

"Does that mean you'll do it? You'll volunteer?" Jessica pressed excitedly.

"I never said that. I'll have to think about it a little longer."

"You're the one who's always saying people should give more of themselves," Jessica wheedled. "Besides, think how much fun it'll be—and we might even learn something."

27

Elizabeth gave in with a laugh. "OK, you win. Honestly, Jess, I think you'd make a better lawyer than Dad. You could probably talk a statue to life if you tried hard enough."

With a squeal, Jessica threw her arms around her sister. "You won't be sorry, Liz! You'll see! It'll be terrific doing it together!"

Elizabeth shook her head. "I don't know how you manage to talk me into these things," she said, but she was smiling. Part of the reason she always found it so hard to say no to Jessica was because she really loved her sister. Despite her occasional dirty tricks, Jessica really was a lot of fun. And maybe there was a serious side to Jessica that Elizabeth had never been aware of before. It certainly was generous of her to want to volunteer her time for such a worthwhile cause. Maybe there was hope for Jessica yet.

Jessica kissed her sister's cheek. "Liz, I don't know what I'd do without you. You're absolutely the best sister in the whole wide world!"

But Jessica wasn't really thinking about Elizabeth at that moment. Her mind was on Jeremy Frank. She pictured herself at his bedside, clasping his hand while he gazed up at her in grateful adoration. In her fantasy she'd just saved his life. Someone had given him the wrong medication, and he would have died if she hadn't called the nurse in time. Jeremy was so grateful that he was practically begging her to be a guest on his show.

"Sounds like a good idea," Mr. Wakefield said at the dinner table after the girls had explained their plan. "I'm all for anything that keeps you out of trouble." He winked to show he was only kidding.

"It'll be a wonderful experience," Mrs. Wakefield put in. "I learned so much the year I was a candy striper." She sighed. "It seems like yesterday. I can hardly believe I have daughters that age now."

It was easy to imagine Alice Wakefield as a teenager. She didn't look much older than the twins, with whom she shared the same sunny blond hair and blue-green eyes. Though she worked as an interior designer, her lithe, tanned figure showed that she spent as much time outdoors as possible.

"We're going to the hospital after school tomorrow to sign up," Jessica said. "When I called the personnel office, the woman said they're really short of volunteers right now and they could use the extra help. The more the merrier, she said. Wow, think of all the people we'll be helping!" But there was one person in particular Jessica was thinking of.

"It's not all fun," Mrs. Wakefield said. "Some of it's hard work. I don't want to spoil your excitement, but I think you should know what to expect."

Jessica frowned, but Elizabeth was quick to say, "A little hard work isn't going to kill us, Mom."

Jessica brightened. "Sure. The more you do for people, the more they appreciate you."

Mrs. Wakefield laughed. "Not always. I'll bet you didn't notice I cleaned up your room, did you, Jess?"

"It would take a week of cleaning before anyone would notice the difference," Elizabeth teased.

Jessica's room was a sore spot, and the butt of many jokes in the Wakefield house. Besides being in a constant state of uproar, Jessica had painted it in a hideous brown color, earning it the nickname of "The Hershey Bar." To Elizabeth it looked more like a mud-wrestling pit crossed with a rummage sale.

"Thanks, Mom," Jessica said sweetly, ignoring her sister's comment. "From now on I promise to keep it neat as a pin all on my own." When she became a television star they might want to interview her in her own house, the way Barbara Walters did, so she might as well get into practice keeping it presentable.

Elizabeth groaned. This was too much! Jessica was becoming so nice she no longer seemed like herself. It seemed too good to be true. Elizabeth couldn't help feeling the tiniest bit suspicious.

"By the way, Dad," Jessica said, "I heard about the new family that's moving into the Godfrey mansion. Is it true?"

Mr. Wakefield smiled. "Word sure travels fast in this town. Well, I guess it's no secret. The deal is closed. The Morrows are planning to move in next week."

"What are they like?" Elizabeth asked.

"So far the only one I've met is Mr. Morrow," he said. "You may be interested to know that our humble town is about to acquire a genuine celebrity."

"I've never heard of him," Jessica said.

"Kurt Morrow played football for the Hawks at one time," he told her. "He was their star quarterback."

"I thought you said he was in the computer business," Mrs. Wakefield put in.

"He is now. Started up his own company a few years ago and it really skyrocketed. Made him a millionaire several times over."

Jessica perked up. "Really? What else do you know? I heard they have a son the same age as Steve."

"They also have a daughter your age. I'm sure you'll be meeting her soon. She's going to Sweet Valley High."

Now Jessica was really intrigued. Between Jeremy Frank and the Morrows, life in Sweet Valley was getting more interesting by the minute.

Four

The following day after school, Elizabeth and Jessica drove over to Joshua Fowler Memorial Hospital. Both girls were silent as they parked the car in front and walked inside. Elizabeth couldn't help remembering how close she'd come to dying in this place after the motorcycle accident she'd been in with Todd. She'd lain in a coma for days. She shuddered at the memory.

At the same time Jessica was thinking about when Annie Whitman had tried to commit suicide after she hadn't made the cheerleading squad. Fortunately she survived, but Jessica never passed by this hospital without feeling a twinge of guilt. She remembered how agonizing it had been to admit that she was just a teensy bit responsible for driving Annie to it.

A plump, middle-aged woman named Mrs. Simpson greeted the twins at the front desk, on the main floor, then took them on a tour. "A lot of people look down their noses at volunteer work," she told them as they followed her down the spotless linoleum corridor. "But in a hospital this size, everybody's job is important, no matter how small. I like to think of Fowler Memorial as a big clock. If one little part breaks down, the whole clock stops running."

"Gee, and I don't even own a watch," Jessica whispered to Elizabeth.

Elizabeth nudged her sister in the ribs to make her keep quiet.

The twins would be responsible for supplying the patients with nonmedical needs such as liquid refreshment, books, and magazines, as well as handling the gift and notions cart. They would also be expected to do some light clerical work and whatever other small tasks the nurses assigned them. Often it would be running errands or just keeping someone company. A lot of the patients were lonely and needed someone to talk with, Mrs. Simpson explained. The nurses were usually too busy to stop and chat for long, but a candy striper's time was more flexible.

Jessica knew exactly which lonely patient she intended to spend her time with. *Her* first job would be finding out which room Jeremy Frank was in. Meanwhile, as the personnel director droned on, Jessica kept busy scouting the hallways for handsome doctors.

When the tour was over, Mrs. Simpson gave them a stack of hospital literature to read at home and told them where they could pick up their uniforms. They would be on a flexible schedule, working two different afternoons every week, starting the next day after school.

Elizabeth was excited as they drove home. "You were right, Jess. We really will be doing some good. Did you see that poor old man sitting out in the hallway in his wheelchair? He looked like he could use some cheering up."

"Ummmm," Jessica responded distractedly. She was daydreaming about Jeremy Frank, imagining that he was holding a microphone in front of her and saying, "Tell us, Jessica, what's it like being a celebrity at the age of sixteen?"

But the next day Jessica was disappointed to learn she'd been assigned to the maternity ward. No chance of running into Jeremy there. She trailed dispiritedly after Mrs. Simpson, who showed her around the ward, then introduced her to the head nurse, Miss North, a grim-faced woman who reminded Jessica of a marine sergeant. Miss North glowered at Jessica from under a heavy shelf of gray eyebrows.

"Do you know anything about babies?" she asked.

"Uh—well, not exactly. Except that I used to be one myself." Jessica smiled disarmingly, hoping to win the head nurse over with a small dose of humor.

Miss North didn't seem to find her remark funny in the least. If anything, she glowered even more fiercely. "I hope you take your job seriously, Miss Wakefield," she snapped. "Because *I* certainly do."

Jessica flushed. "Uh, sure I do." *Help!* she thought.

"Good. You can start with this then." Miss North handed her a bulging white plastic garbage bag.

"What is it?" Jessica asked.

"Dirty diapers," she barked in reply, pointing the way toward the disposal unit.

From then on it seemed to grow progressively worse. Jessica's next chore was finding a vase for a bouquet that had arrived for one of the new mothers. When she brought the flowers into the room, she noticed that the woman was holding her baby.

She beamed up at Jessica. "Isn't he the most adorable baby you've ever seen?"

Jessica stared down at the squirming red bundle on the bed. It was working itself up into a -fury, waving its fists, opening and closing its toothless mouth like a fish.

Jessica gulped. "Absolutely," she lied.

She spent the remainder of the hour telling

the same lie to every new mother who thrust a baby or a photo of one into her face. She must have looked at a dozen before it was time to take a break. Jessica took the elevator upstairs to look for Elizabeth, who had been assigned to the second floor. She found her sister wheeling her cart past the nurses' station.

"Save any lives yet?" Elizabeth teased, her eyes sparkling.

"Ugh! Are you kidding? All I did was look at a million Polaroids of babies."

"It doesn't sound so bad," Elizabeth said.

"How'd you make out?" Jessica asked. She helped herself to a cup of orange juice from the cart.

"Great! Listen, Jess, this is the best idea you ever had. I've met a lot of interesting people so far. I'm even thinking of asking Mr. Collins if I can do a piece for *The Oracle* on it. Do you know who I met when I was passing around magazines?"

"Let me guess. Some fascinating old man who told you all about how he fought in the Civil War, right?" Jessica yawned.

Elizabeth grinned. "Hardly."

"OK, I give up. Tell me who."

"Jeremy Frank. He's in two-thirteen."

"Jeremy Frank! You *saw* him? You actually saw him?"

"Sure. We even talked. He's nice."

Jessica was clutching her chest. "I can't believe you actually talked to Jeremy Frank. What did you talk about?" Of all the unfair things— Elizabeth had gotten to see him first!

Elizabeth shrugged. "Um, let me see. . . . We talked about his show mostly. I told him I really liked it and that I was thinking of majoring in journalism when I went to college. Then he thanked me."

"He thanked you? What for? You didn't kiss him, did you?"

Elizabeth laughed. "No, I didn't kiss him. Honestly, Jess, where do you get such strange ideas? All I did was get him a glass of water. He was thirsty. It was no big deal."

"Not to you maybe," Jessica muttered.

"Oh, sure, I know he's a big celebrity and all, but I don't see any reason to start acting weird about it. He's probably sick of people who treat him like he's some kind of god. He's just as human as anyone else. In fact, right now he doesn't look like much of a celebrity with his leg in a cast sticking up in the air."

"Didn't you even ask him for his autograph?"

"No." Elizabeth smiled. "I did give him *my* autograph, though. He asked me to sign his cast—in case I turned out to be someone famous someday. Jess!" She grabbed her sister's arm. Jessica looked positively green. "Jess, what's the matter? Are you sick?"

Jessica swallowed. "Listen, Liz, do you think they'd let me change wards? I think the one

I've been working on might be contagious. Maybe I could help you out on this one."

Elizabeth laughed. "Gosh, I hope it isn't contagious. You *did* say it was the maternity ward, didn't you?"

Jessica shot her sister a dirty look. "Very funny." Trying to sound casual, she asked, "Hey, by the way, what room did you say Jeremy was in?"

"Two-thirteen. Why do you—?" Elizabeth stopped as realization dawned. "Jessica, you're not thinking what I think you're thinking. Give the poor man a break! He's sick. He needs rest. What he *doesn't* need is you."

"Why, Liz, I can't imagine what you could possibly mean," Jessica replied innocently. "I only want to see what he looks like in person. That's all. Just a tiny peek."

"Why don't I believe you?" Elizabeth said and groaned.

Once Jessica had a certain male in her sights, Elizabeth knew there was no stopping her. She would do anything to get him. In Jeremy's case, Elizabeth could certainly see the attraction. He was awfully cute. If she weren't so much in love with Todd, she might even be attracted to him herself. The other problem, of course, was that Jeremy was too old. Mid-twenties at least. Their mom and dad would flip if they knew Jessica was chasing after a man that age!

Jessica was frowning in annoyance. "It's so

39

unfair. I'm stuck downstairs with a lot of screaming babies, and you're living it up with Jeremy Frank. If I'd known how it was going to be, I never would have—'' She stopped, realizing she'd said too much.

Elizabeth's eyes narrowed. "You *knew*, didn't you? You knew all along that Jeremy Frank was here with a broken leg. *That's* why you wanted to be a candy striper! All that talk about making sacrifices and doing good deeds for the sake of mankind. I can't believe I swallowed it!"

Jessica edged around to the other side of the cart. "You've got it all wrong, Liz." She darted a strategic glance at the clock over the nurses' station. "Listen, I've got to run. My time's up. Sorry." She crumpled her paper cup and tossed it into a wastebasket on her way to the elevator. "Talk to you later!" she called.

Elizabeth sighed. Once again she'd been had by her sister. Except this time she really didn't mind so much. However selfish Jessica's motives had been, the results were good. Elizabeth was glad she'd volunteered for this job. The work was fun and interesting, and it was only for a few hours a week, so it really wasn't going to take up too much of her time. Only one problem remained. She'd have to find a way of warning Jeremy that Hurricane Jessica was on her way.

Elizabeth was so wrapped up in her thoughts as she pushed her cart down the corridor that she didn't see the dark-haired orderly who had stopped to look at her. But she was alerted by the loud crash as the tray he was carrying slid from his grasp.

Elizabeth rushed over to help him pick everything up. As she bent down, she noticed his hands were trembling. Poor guy! Maybe he was afraid of losing his job, or maybe he was just embarrassed at appearing so clumsy. She smiled reassuringly at him.

"Don't worry. It was an accident," she said sweetly. "Anyway, I know what it's like. I'm always dropping things."

The orderly was short and husky, about twenty-five or so, with a hawkish nose and the darkest eyes Elizabeth had ever seen. At the moment they were fixed on her with an intensity that sent a rash of goosebumps skittering up her spine. Why was he staring at her like that?

"I'm Elizabeth," she said when he didn't respond. "This is my first day here."

He nodded. "My name is Carl," he said in a low, husky voice, as if having to speak were painful. Elizabeth felt sorry for him. He was probably just terribly shy.

She reached over to retrieve a paper cup that had rolled out of his reach. When she handed it to him, their fingers touched briefly. Elizabeth experienced a cold shock. As the man hurried off, she couldn't help thinking that there was something strange about him. Or was it just her writer's imagination getting out of hand again? She tried to push her thoughts of him out of her mind as she went back to her cart and continued down the long hospital corridor.

She was nearing the end of the ward when she spotted someone up ahead who looked familiar. Though it was a warm day, the girl was bundled in a heavy sweater. Her head was tucked low, but there was no mistaking the bright cloud of strawberry-blond hair that floated about her hunched shoulders.

"Tricia!" Elizabeth called out.

Tricia Martin paused and looked up, her eyes wide as a startled deer's as she recognized Elizabeth. Then, with a furtive expression, she scurried ahead without a word of hello, vanishing around the corner.

What was Tricia doing here? Elizabeth wondered. And why had she run away like that? Did she think the whole Wakefield family was against her because of Steven? Or—an ugly thought intruded—had she been visiting someone she didn't want Steven to know about? A new boyfriend, perhaps? A lot of the orderlies who worked here were Steven's age.

One thing puzzled Elizabeth more than anything else. It was clear to her, even after a brief glance, that Tricia was no happier than Steven was these days. In fact, she looked truly awful, as if she hadn't slept or eaten in a week. She'd lost weight, and there were dark smudges under her eyes.

The breakup had been Tricia's idea, but she certainly did seem miserable.

Jessica paused outside the door to Room 213. She'd doubled back up the stairs after leaving the elevator. Now she glanced about furtively to make sure Elizabeth was nowhere in sight. Satisfied, she pushed her way inside.

The first thing that caught her eye was a huge plaster cast suspended in midair by a system of cables and pulleys.

"Did you forget something?" asked a pleasantly deep voice.

Jessica's gaze shifted to the tanned, angular face resting against the pillow. Jeremy Frank's ice-blue eyes sparkled at her, and his mouth was curved up in a smile, revealing deep dimples that creased his cheeks all the way to his jawline. Jessica noticed there was also a darling cleft in the middle of his chin. Jeremy Frank was definitely better-looking in person than he was on TV. Jessica was struck speechless for a moment.

"You were in here a few minutes ago," he prompted. "Elizabeth isn't it?"

Jessica cleared her throat. "You're thinking of my sister. She's Elizabeth. I'm Jessica."

His smile broadened. "Twins."

"Identical," Jessica chirped. "That is, we *look*

43

exactly alike, but if you want to know the truth, Elizabeth is a lot shyer—almost a hermit sometimes. I have to work at getting her to come out of her shell. But that's OK, 'cause I love helping people. That's why I volunteered for this job." She shot him a dazzling grin. "Can I get you a drink of water?"

"Thanks, but I've had plenty."

Jessica tried to hide her disappointment. "Isn't there anything I can do for you?"

"I can't think of anything right now. Except" —he picked up a pen from his bedside table— "you can return this to your sister. She left it here when she signed my cast."

"Can I sign it, too?" she asked, not to be outdone by her twin.

"Sure thing." He handed her the pen. "Don't tell me you're a writer like your sister."

Jessica dimpled. "Nothing that boring. I'm going to be an actress. A *TV* actress," she hinted outrageously.

"I see," Jeremy said, stifling a smile.

Jessica's heart beat quickly as she held the pen poised over his cast, looking for a spot that wasn't already written on or decorated. As she leaned forward, she lost her balance. Instinctively she put out her right hand and hit him in his other kneecap, jabbing it with the pen. Jeremy let out a yelp, jerking upright so suddenly that one of the cables holding his leg up was pulled loose. He groaned loudly, his face as white as the sheets he was lying on.

Speechless with horror, Jessica could only stare at him.

"Get . . . a . . . nurse," he croaked.

"A nurse. Sure. I'll be right back. Don't go anywhere."

"Where would I go?" he mumbled weakly.

Jessica dashed out of the room. Her one chance at stardom and she'd probably blown it for good! She found a nurse and managed to babble out what had happened. The nurse shot Jessica a disgusted look before bustling off in the direction of Jeremy's room.

Jessica sank down on a chair in the waiting room. Maybe it wasn't completely hopeless, she told herself. Maybe there was still a chance of showing Jeremy how devoted she could be, of earning his undying gratitude—and a guest spot on his show.

Five

"I'm not in the mood for a party," Steven growled. "Thanks, Jess, but I'll pass."

"But, Steve!" Jessica dropped down beside her brother, who lay sprawled on the living room couch. It was Friday, and he'd just arrived home for the weekend. "It would be so much fun. Besides, Cara's feelings would be hurt if you couldn't come."

"Cara Walker, huh?" Steven shot her a wise look. "I think I know what this is all about. Look, if you're trying to fix me up with her again, you can forget it."

Jessica stuck out her lower lip. "How can you be so mean? I was only trying to do you a favor. I know how bad you're feeling about Tricia. I thought a party might cheer you up."

Steven's expression softened. "Well, it was a nice thought, but I don't think anything could cheer me up right now."

He went back to peering glumly at the history textbook he'd been trying to read without much success. Forgetting Tricia was proving to be an impossible task. He felt as heartsick about the whole thing as he had the night they broke up.

But Jessica wasn't giving up as easily as that. "You can't just mope around forever. You have your reputation to think of."

"I don't get the connection," Steven said in bewilderment. "What's my reputation got to do with it?"

"You don't want people to start thinking you're a wimp, do you? Only wimps sit around doing their homework on Friday night when they could be out partying."

Steven shrugged. He wasn't the least bit interested in his reputation, Jessica could see. He looked awful, too, as if he hadn't eaten or slept all week—which he probably hadn't. Getting him to stop thinking about Tricia wasn't going to be as easy as she'd hoped. Jessica leaned over and planted an affectionate kiss on her brother's unshaven cheek.

"Come on, Steve, don't be stubborn. You could go just for an hour or so. If you don't have fun, you can always leave. It would mean *so* much to Cara."

"I see we're back to Cara again."

"And what's wrong with Cara, I'd like to know?" Jessica shot back indignantly. "Honestly, the way you're acting, anyone would think she had two heads and weighed three hundred pounds. In case you haven't noticed lately, Cara happens to be fantastic-looking."

"Great. Then she should have no trouble getting dates on her own."

Jessica resisted the impulse to bat him over the head with a pillow. Instead, she tried to catch him with some different bait.

"I'll bet Tricia's not going to be sitting home tonight," she suggested slyly.

At the mention of Tricia's name, Steven slammed his book shut and scowled up at Jessica. "What makes you such an expert on Tricia all of a sudden?" he demanded angrily.

"Oh, I don't know. I hear things around school—you know how it is." Jessica yawned, pretending to be bored with the whole subject.

"Like what things?" he persisted.

"Well, Cara told me just the other day that she heard from one of the seniors that Tricia's been cutting an awful lot of classes lately."

Steven's frown deepened. "That doesn't sound like Tricia. She's always been an A student."

"Maybe she found something better to do. You remember what happened with Betsy after

48

she started hanging around with that dropout Rick Andover. It wasn't long before she was flunking half her classes."

"Tricia's not like Betsy," Steven insisted stubbornly.

"I don't see how you can defend her after the way she treated you! If you ask me, she *deserves* to flunk out."

"What else did Cara say about Tricia?" Steven asked.

Jessica suppressed a smile of triumph. The bait had worked. He was hooked. Now all she had to do was reel him in.

"How on earth would *I* know? I'm not the FBI. Of course, if you're *really* interested, you could always ask Cara yourself."

"Who says you're not the FBI? Only in your case it stands for Forever Butting In." Giving a weary sigh, Steven rose from the couch. "What time did you say the party was?"

Jessica had to stand on tiptoe to hug him. "Eight-thirty. And don't worry—you won't regret this, Steve. Cross my heart!"

"I think I'm already regretting it."

But Jessica wasn't listening. She was dashing upstairs to phone Cara.

"You told him I was having a party? Tonight?" Cara shrieked into the phone. "Jessica Wakefield, how *could* you? He'll think I'm the biggest creep in Sweet Valley when he gets here and finds out it was all a big lie!"

"I had to tell him *something*," Jessica said. "Would you rather I told him you were madly in love with him and were dying for a date?"

"You wouldn't dare!"

"OK, so it's not the greatest plan in the world, but it was the best I could come up with. Just put some potato chips out and we'll invite a few more people. I didn't tell him it was going to be a *big* party."

"Who can we invite at the last minute?"

"Well, I could ask Liz and Todd. I'll tell Liz I'm doing it for Steve. It's the truth. I'm just making sure he doesn't go running back to that no-good Tricia." She sighed. "The trouble is, no one around here seems to care about the Wakefield reputation except me."

"Gee, that's tough, Jess," Cara said, not bothering to hide the sarcasm in her voice. "What I want to know is what you're going to do about *me*. What if you can't get anyone to come?"

"You can always pretend you invited a bunch of people but no one showed up."

"Great. Then I'll look like the biggest nerd this side of the Rockies." Cara moaned loudly. "How did I ever let you talk me into this?"

"Just leave everything to me," Jessica said confidently.

"Do I have a choice?"

"Sure. You can always back out. Then some other lucky girl will probably snag Steven."

There was a brief silence at the other end. "Well, when you put it that way . . ."

Jessica laughed. "Trust me, Cara. You won't be sorry. Just put on the sexiest outfit you own. Nature will take care of the rest. Don't forget, Steve's only human."

Six

"Hi, everybody! Hi, Steve! I'm really glad you could come."

Cara greeted them at the door. She was wearing a splashy Hawaiian-print halter dress. It was cut so low in back that Steven could see the white lines from her bikini crisscrossing her dark tan. She had pulled her long brown hair into a ponytail over one ear so that it snaked seductively down her bare shoulder.

From the moment he saw Cara, Steven was sorry he'd come. It was a mistake. He never should have let Jessica talk him into this. It was an effort to control the sudden urge he had to run to the nearest phone and call Tricia.

What was she doing right then? Who was she with?

Anger pounded in his temples, and his face grew hot at the thought of Tricia with someone else. He'd spent the entire week trying to make himself hate her, but it was no good. Each time he pictured her—golden-haired and fragile, with those great misty blue eyes—he wanted to take her in his arms, to protect her from—

From what? he asked himself. Tricia didn't want his love or his protection. She'd told him so herself. Yet there had been something about her, something that twisted his heart at the memory of how she'd looked the night of their breakup. As if she still loved him. As if what she was saying had hurt her more than it was hurting him.

He knew he was probably just imagining it because he wanted so much for it to be true. A part of him still didn't believe she could end it like that. You couldn't stop loving someone just like shutting off a faucet. At least he couldn't.

At first he'd been so angry at Tricia that he couldn't see straight, but lately he'd been remembering all the good times they'd had together. Tricia's presence in his life had been like the sun and the moon and the stars all rolled into one.

"Looks like we're practically the first ones to get here," Jessica commented as she looked about the nearly deserted living room. Only one other

53

couple had arrived so far. She waved to Lila Fowler, who was sitting on the couch talking to her date, a boy Jessica didn't recognize.

Cara blushed. "Uh, well . . . a bunch of people called and said they couldn't make it."

"Don't worry," Jessica assured Cara. "I think it's much nicer this way. I hate big parties. They're so noisy. This is much more intimate." She turned to her date, handsome soccer player Aaron Dallas. Don't you agree, Aaron?"

"Sure do." Grinning, he put an arm about her waist. "I like intimate parties, too. The more intimate, the better."

Steven winced as he watched his sister plant a kiss on Aaron's waiting cheek. Jessica probably didn't know the meaning of real love, he thought. She wouldn't understand the way he felt about Tricia, what it was like to love someone so much you couldn't imagine life without that person.

"Where are Liz and Todd?" Cara asked, beginning to show signs of nervousness.

Jessica shrugged. "They couldn't make it. Todd had some concert tickets." She didn't want to tell Cara the truth—that Elizabeth had simply refused to have any part in fixing her up with Steven.

"I didn't know there was a concert tonight," Lila put in. "What group is playing?"

"It's—nobody you ever heard of," Jessica hedged. She felt like kicking Lila.

Lila laughed, tossing her head so that her wavy, light brown hair rippled across her shoulders. "Believe me, Jessica, there isn't a group I *haven't* heard of."

The Fowlers were so rich that Lila had her own built-in stereo system in her bedroom, with a record collection that stretched wall to wall.

Jessica could feel herself growing warm. "Uh, it's a classical group," she finally said. "You know how crazy Liz is about all that highbrow stuff."

Lila wrinkled her nose in distaste. "Classical music just puts me to sleep."

Her date, a preppy type with short, rust-red hair and devilish blue eyes, said, "No sleep tonight, Lila. I've got other plans."

"Oh, Jim!" Lila giggled, pretending to be shocked, but she didn't pull away when he hooked an arm about her shoulder, drawing her in for a kiss.

"Speaking of big plans," Cara interrupted, "I just found out about a party you won't want to miss."

Jessica frowned. Usually she knew about every party of any importance long before invitations were made. "Who's giving it?"

"Regina Morrow. You know, the new girl who's moving into the Godfrey mansion. I haven't met her yet, but my mother met her mother. That's how I found out. It's going to be a kind of get-to-know-everyone party. She's inviting the whole junior class. She's going all out, too. It's supposed to be really fancy. I guess she wants to make a good impression."

"Wow!" Jessica's blue-green eyes sparkled with enthusiasm. "I can't wait!"

"I thought you didn't like big parties," Aaron teased.

Jessica blushed, casting a guilty glance at Cara, who was glaring at her across the room. For once, Jessica was speechless.

Cara ducked into the kitchen and came out carrying a six-pack of beer. "My parents aren't home," she explained with a sheepish smile.

Steven shook his head when she offered him a beer. He didn't feel like drinking. He didn't feel much like talking to anyone either. All he wanted was to be with Tricia. Nibbling listlessly at a potato chip, he sank down on the couch.

"Don't be such a party pooper, Steve!" Jessica sang out as Cara put a record on the turntable.

The room thundered with a pulsing beat. Jessica and Aaron started to whirl across the carpet with their arms looped about each other's waists. Then they disappeared outside, and Steven could hear their laughter drifting in from the darkened patio. A few minutes later, Lila and her date joined them.

Cara curled up next to Steven on the couch. She kicked her sandals off, tucking her feet up underneath her. She wasted no time in getting directly to the point.

"I heard you and Tricia broke up," she said. "That's too bad. Tricia's a nice girl." She didn't sound very sincere.

Steven found himself asking, almost against his will, "How well do you know Tricia? Uh . . . I was just wondering if you ever talked or anything."

He hated himself immediately. Why should he care one way or another if they were friends? It was over between Tricia and him. She had made that crystal clear. Why torture himself?

"I don't really know her that well," Cara admitted. "Tricia's—well, you could call her the shy type."

Steven recalled Elizabeth telling him once that Cara Walker was the biggest gossip in school. Maybe Tricia had been reluctant to get close to Cara for that reason. Tricia had enough to worry about as it was without a gossipmonger spreading even more stories about her family.

"Anyway," Cara went on, "you don't have to worry about hurting her feelings anymore. Jessica told me it was your idea to break up, but I guess Tricia must have gotten over it in a big hurry."

"What do you mean?" Steven asked slowly. There was a roaring in his ears, and his mouth was so dry he could hardly swallow.

"I heard she's got a new boyfriend," Cara

replied, dropping her voice to a confidential whisper.

Steve fought to keep his emotions under control. "Oh? Somebody from school?"

"I don't think so. Caroline didn't recognize him. That's who I heard it from—Caroline Pearce. She said she saw Tricia and this guy down at the drugstore a couple of days ago. According to Caroline, Tricia was draped all over him."

Steven felt himself stiffen. "Yeah, well, it's none of my business what she does. We're not going together anymore."

"That's what I told Caroline."

"Tricia can see whoever she wants."

"I couldn't agree with you more, Steve," Cara cooed.

"I mean, if she wants to hang all over some creep in public, what's it to me?"

"Absolutely nothing. Steve, what are you getting so excited about?"

"I'm not excited!" he practically roared. Abruptly he grabbed Cara's wrist, pulling her to her feet. "Let's dance. I feel like dancing." *To hell with Tricia*, he thought, but that didn't stop his eyes from stinging with unshed tears.

Cara smiled dreamily. "Sure, Steve, whatever you say."

The song now playing was soft and dreamy. Stiffly Steven placed his arms around Cara. With a sigh of contentment, she melted against him. Steven closed his eyes, imagining it was Tricia he was holding. Tricia's warm body pressed so closely to his, Tricia's fingertips dancing lightly over the back of his neck—

Stop it! he commanded himself. He was thinking like an idiot. Some other guy was probably holding Tricia right now, kissing her, maybe even telling her he loved her.

Suddenly Steven jerked his head forward and kissed Cara hard on the lips. But he felt nothing. Just cold inside. Cold and dead.

Cara stirred eagerly in his arms. "Oh, Steve," she murmured. "I think this is going to be the nicest party I ever had."

Jessica smirked as she bounced down on Elizabeth's bed. It was past one, and she'd just returned from Cara's party. "I hate to say I told you so. Steve didn't need much encouraging. He was all *over* Cara!"

Elizabeth sat up and blinked. She'd just been dozing off when Jessica came barging in. "I don't believe it," she said.

"Ask Lila. She was there. She saw the way Steve was acting." Jessica smiled as she began peeling off her pantyhose. "I don't think we need to worry about Steve mourning over Tricia anymore. He's probably forgotten her name by now."

Elizabeth still couldn't quite believe it. What could have happened to make Steven change his mind about Cara so quickly? Knowing Jessica and her tricks, it could have been *anything*.

"Do you think it's serious?" she asked.

Jessica's smile broadened. "I hope so. Steve didn't even come home with me. He and Cara must be off in some cozy place right this minute."

"Come on, Jess, you *can't* mean it. Cara's all wrong for Steve."

"What do you have against Cara?" Jessica demanded. "She's cute, and she's popular—and she's even on the cheering squad."

"Well, if she's on the cheering squad than she *must* be the perfect girl," Elizabeth commented dryly.

"Who cares about perfect? Being *fun* is what counts with guys. Steve deserves to have some fun after being around Miss Goody-Goody Martin for so long."

Sighing, Elizabeth sank back on her pillow. "I just hope Steve knows what he's doing."

It was almost two o'clock in the morning by the time Steven arrived home. He and Cara had gone out for a pizza, and then she'd insisted they drive around for a while. He got the feeling she was more interested in being *seen* with him than actually being with him.

He was tired, but he knew he wouldn't be able to sleep. He headed for the kitchen. Maybe a cup of hot cocoa would make him feel better.

He'd really tried to have a good time, but it was no use, he thought as he got out the cocoa powder. The more he tried to stop thinking about Tricia, the worse it got. She was on his mind constantly. He couldn't forget her any more than he could forget there was a sun in the sky.

Mr. Wakefield came downstairs in his bathrobe as Steven was heating the cocoa.

"Thought I heard someone rattling around down here," he said. "Hey, is there enough for two?"

Steven looked up. "Sure, Dad."

"I remember when you were little your mother always made you hot cocoa when you were upset about something."

Steven forced a weak smile. "The problems I had then seem so small compared to now."

Mr. Wakefield placed a hand on his son's shoulder. "Want to tell me about it?"

Steven felt a rush of warmth toward his father. There was a kinship between them that went much deeper than physical likeness. But Steven was certain this was one time when even his father couldn't help.

Steven shrugged as he poured the cocoa into cups. "There isn't much to tell. Tricia wants out. It's as simple as that."

"I know how tough this is for you, Steve."

Steven swallowed, unable to speak. There was

a huge lump in his throat. Finally he said, "I'll be OK, Dad. I just need time, I guess."

Mr. Wakefield took the cup Steven held out to him and sat down to drink his cocoa. "How did it go at the party tonight?"

Steven smiled ruefully. "It wasn't exactly what I expected, let's put it that way."

Cara's words played over and over inside his mind—*Tricia's got a new boyfriend*. Each time it was like a knife digging into his heart.

His father nodded sympathetically. "I think I get the picture. Just one word of advice: I know your sister means well, but don't let her push you into anything you're not ready for, OK?"

"OK, Dad."

There was no sense trying to explain how he was feeling. He hardly understood it himself. What difference did it make if he went on dating Cara? No matter what he did, he'd never get over Tricia.

Seven

On Monday Elizabeth was on her way to the cafeteria to meet Todd for lunch when she passed Tricia, sitting alone on the lawn. She was staring off into space, the sandwich in her hand untouched. She looked so miserable that Elizabeth couldn't help feeling sorry for her, despite the way she'd treated Steven.

On impulse, Elizabeth went over and sat down beside her. "Tricia," she blurted out, "what's going on? Why did you run away from me at the hospital?"

Tricia's cheeks flooded with color, and she dropped her gaze. "I'm sorry, Liz. It was rude of me, I know. I—I just didn't feel like talking to anyone right then. I was . . . visiting someone. A friend of mine. I was pretty upset."

"Is your friend really sick?"

The corners of Tricia's mouth twisted upward in a brief, sad smile. "I guess you could say that."

"Maybe I've met her," Elizabeth said. "I just started working as a candy striper, but I know a lot of the patients. What room is she in?"

"You wouldn't know her. S-she checked out," Tricia stammered.

"She must be feeling better then," Elizabeth said. "That's great."

Tricia shrugged. "It's one of those in-and-out things. You know, in for a couple of days of treatment, then out again."

Elizabeth nodded sympathetically. "What's wrong with her?"

"She told me, but I can't remember. One of those unpronounceable things no one's ever heard of."

"Well, I hope it's not too serious."

Abruptly Tricia changed the subject. "Do you want my sandwich, Liz? I'm not hungry."

Elizabeth shook her head. "I'm meeting Todd for lunch. Want to join us?"

"Thanks," Tricia said, "but I—I have some studying to catch up on."

Elizabeth was close to saying something about Steven, but she decided against it. Tricia had been friendly, but it was obvious she preferred to be alone. Whatever was bothering her, it was something too deep and private to share. Her eyes were bloodshot, and she looked thin, too, as if she hadn't been getting enough to eat. At that moment Tricia reminded Elizabeth of a very fragile china figurine.

Wishing there was something more she could do, but not knowing what, Elizabeth stood up and brushed loose bits of grass from her jeans. "Well, I guess I'd better get going. Todd will wonder what happened to me."

Just as Elizabeth was saying goodbye, Cara and Jessica walked up. They saw Tricia and exchanged knowing looks.

"Hi, Liz," Cara greeted cheerily, ignoring Tricia. "Gee, it was too bad you couldn't make it to my party. It was a real blast."

"Todd and I had something else to do," Elizabeth said stiffly. "You should have let us know sooner."

"Well, it was one of those spur-of-the-moment things," Cara replied with a sparkling little laugh. "I don't know when I've had so much fun! I'll bet you didn't know what a fantastic dancer your brother is, Liz."

Elizabeth glanced quickly at Tricia, then back up at Cara. Tricia pretended not to have heard, but it was obvious she had. Burning red flags of humiliation scorched her pale cheeks.

"I guess there's a lot I don't know about

Steve," Elizabeth said, trying to keep her voice even.

Cara giggled, tossing a triumphant look in Tricia's direction. "I'll bet he didn't tell you he's taking me to one of his college parties next weekend," she said.

"No, he didn't," Elizabeth said softly.

"You know Steve," Jessica put in. "Always so darn secretive about his love life."

Love life! Elizabeth thought. Since when had Cara become a part of Steve's love life? Suddenly furious, she commented coldly, "Maybe he's being secretive because he has something to be ashamed of!"

She brushed past angrily, leaving them to gape after her in astonishment. Elizabeth rarely lost her temper, but when she did, even Jessica knew enough to step out of the way.

"I can't imagine what's gotten into her," Elizabeth heard her sister muttering to Cara as she stalked off.

Elizabeth cast a last glance over her shoulder at Tricia. *Poor Tricia!* She was sitting still as a statue, a smile frozen on her lips. But her eyes betrayed the emotion she was feeling. They were huge and sad, glittering with tears. What was she thinking? Elizabeth wondered.

It's better this way, Tricia repeated to herself, as she'd been doing all week. *Better for Steve that he's found someone else.*

But she couldn't stop the cold feeling in her chest, as if an icicle lay wedged alongside her heart. She couldn't seem to stop the tears either. They dripped silently onto the backs of her hands, clasped tightly in her lap. The world that had been so unbearably sharp a moment before had blurred, and the voices around her faded to a distant buzzing.

The drugs she was taking sometimes made her sick to her stomach, but she wasn't sick now, just tired and very, very cold. She shivered in the warm sunlight, hugging her arms. She felt so alone, so desperately alone. *If only Steve could be with me*, she cried to herself. *If only I could feel his strong arms around me just one more time, I could be warm again*.

She knew these were dangerous thoughts, but she couldn't seem to stop them, just as she'd been unable to stop her tears. Images of Steven flashed into her mind. She saw them running along the beach, the wind whipping through their hair. They had run until they were out of breath, then tumbled together onto the sand. She thought of him arriving at the house to pick her up on their first date, greeting her father courteously even though he was so drunk he could hardly stand up. Tricia closed her eyes, remembering how it felt the first time Steven kissed her, cupping her face with one hand as he lightly ran a thumb along her cheek. She'd been trembling so hard she was sure she wouldn't be able to stand up when it was all over.

Steve! Tricia's heart cried out his name, though no sound escaped her lips. *I can't bear to lose you! Without you, I'm already dead!* It would be so simple to let him know how she felt. There was a pay phone right outside the cafeteria. As simple as slipping a dime in the coin slot and dialing his number. She could tell him everything. Maybe it wasn't too late. She could tell him she still loved him.

No! Tricia bit down so hard on her lip she could taste blood. She had to stop thinking this way! It was selfish and cruel to want to make Steven suffer as much as she was suffering. *Let him go*, the voice of reason whispered in her head. *If you love him, let him go.*

Yes, it was better this way. She watched Cara and Jessica stroll off, their heads bent together in whispered conversation. No doubt they were talking about Steven, making plans. Next weekend Cara and Steven would go to the party, and maybe they were going out this coming weekend too. He would forget about her. That was the way it should be. He would be happy again, and soon it wouldn't matter to her either, because in a few months she would be gone.

Eight

"Something strange is going on," Elizabeth said as she set down her tray beside Todd at the cafeteria table.

Todd looked up from his hamburger. He swallowed and said, "That sounds like the opening line of a mystery novel." His brown eyes sparkled with mischief. "Any clues so far, Sherlock?"

"Come on, Todd, I'm serious," Elizabeth answered as she sat down, but she couldn't resist a small smile. Todd was such a kidder. His sense of humor was one of the things she loved best about him—plus about six feet of muscle topped by wavy brown hair and a brilliant white smile. "It's this thing with Steve and Tricia.

69

Steve told me it was Tricia who wanted to break up, but the way she's acting you'd think it was the other way around. I just *know* she's still in love with him. I can feel it, even though she doesn't say so."

"You're too sensitive for your own good," Todd said, tweaking the end of her nose. Then he grew sober. "I know what you mean, though. I have study hall with Tricia, but I don't think she's too interested in studying these days."

"How do you know?"

"I happened to look over her shoulder this morning as I was walking past. She was just staring at this picture of Steve she had tucked inside her binder. It kind of got to me. It was the *way* she was looking at it more than anything. Like"—he lowered his voice—"it's hard to describe, but sort of like Steve was gone or something. Isn't that weird?"

Elizabeth shook her head. "No. I felt that way, too. Todd, what do you think is happening? I know it's none of my business, but I can't help feeling involved. Steve's my brother, and I really like Tricia. It just doesn't seem right, their being apart if they still love each other."

"I agree with you," Todd said. "But what can we do about it? They'd only resent it if we tried to butt in."

Elizabeth sighed. "I'm afraid Jessica's already taken care of that. She's got Steve fixed up with Cara."

Todd dropped his fork. "Cara Walker? You've got to be kidding! Poor Steve! You'd better tell him to watch what he says around her. It could end up in the *National Enquirer*."

"I don't think Steve really likes Cara. He's probably only going out with her to make Tricia jealous." Elizabeth picked listlessly at her food. At least she *hoped* Steven wasn't falling for Cara.

"Have you tried talking to him about it?" Todd asked.

She nodded. "He thinks Tricia has another boyfriend, but I'm not so sure. Why would she be so miserable if she had someone else?"

"You're right. I don't buy it either. Somehow I can't imagine Tricia with anyone but Steve. They seemed so perfect together."

"Like us, you mean?" Elizabeth fed Todd a french fry off her plate, yanking her hand away with an outraged giggle when he began nibbling her fingers.

Todd laughed. "Face it. Nobody is like us. If we were any crazier about each other, they'd have to send out the little men in the white coats."

"You're so romantic, Todd."

Todd kissed her lightly. His lips were a delicious combination of sweet and salty. Elizabeth felt warm all over. No matter how many times he'd kissed her, it always affected her this way. As if he were kissing her for the very first time. Maybe that was why she was so concerned about

Steven and Tricia. She knew what it was like to love someone deeply. The thought of losing Todd was unbearable.

"Maybe you should talk to Tricia," Todd suggested. "You know, woman to woman. Maybe it's something she's too embarrassed to tell Steve."

"I thought of that. I tried talking to her today, but she never mentioned Steve once. Besides, Tricia and I don't really know each other that well. I wouldn't want it to look like I was spying for my brother."

"I doubt if she'd think that. Tell her the truth— that you're just trying to help because you can see how unhappy they both are. Why shouldn't she believe you? Anyone can tell just by looking at you that you're the sincere type."

"You wouldn't happen to be the teeniest bit prejudiced, would you?"

"Me? Not a chance!" Todd grinned before shoveling in the last of his hamburger. "Anyway, my advice is to act fast—before Cara gets her claws in any deeper."

Elizabeth groaned. Todd was right. But what could she do if Tricia wouldn't confide in her? Nothing, that's what. Just sit back and watch her brother and Tricia mess up their lives.

It was an awful thought.

Today is the day, Jessica thought the next afternoon as she slipped into her candy striper's uniform. This time she was really going to make sure Jeremy noticed her.

"Wake up, Jessica," Elizabeth said when her sister didn't get off the elevator on the first floor. "The maternity ward is on *this* floor."

"Uh—I left something upstairs last week," Jessica mumbled, praying the elevator door would close before Miss North caught up with her and forced her into dirty-diaper detail again.

Jessica's heart was pounding as she neared Jeremy's room, but she felt confident she'd be able to get his attention this time. Who knew? Maybe she'd even get a chance to help him for real. Cheered by that thought, she filled a pitcher of water to take with her in case he was thirsty.

She sailed into the room, prepared to win Jeremy over. She glanced toward the bed, frowning slightly as she noticed the nurse standing over him. But she put on her most dazzling smile and continued forward anyway. Jeremy *had* to see her at her best. Jessica came up alongside the nurse—and froze in her tracks.

Jeremy was *stark naked*!

The nurse was giving him a sponge bath, and there he lay without a stitch on. Jessica gave a little yelp, and the pitcher in her hands tipped forward, dumping ice-cold water on Jeremy's bare stomach.

Jeremy roared in pain, nearly hitting the ceiling. He tried to sit up, but his broken leg was suspended too high, and he could only flop helplessly from side to side while the nurse made a frantic attempt to mop up the spillage with her towel.

Finally Jeremy managed to point a finger at Jessica and choke, "You!"

The nurse glared at her. "What are you doing in here? Are you trying to give this man heart failure?"

"I—I was only trying to help," Jessica stammered.

"Help?" both Jeremy and the nurse echoed in unison.

With an injured cry, Jessica turned and fled the room. Did they have to get so upset over a little water? It wasn't her fault, was it? How could she have known it would turn out that way?

"You did *what*?" Elizabeth stared at her sister in horror when Jessica related what had happened.

They were sitting in the nurses' lounge during their break. Elizabeth nearly choked on the oatmeal cookie she was nibbling.

"It wasn't like I did it on purpose!" Jessica cried in self-defense. "I was only trying to help."

"Any more of that kind of help and Jeremy may never get out of this hospital alive," Elizabeth warned.

Jessica smiled tentatively. "Well, at least I got him to notice me. That's a start, isn't it?"

Elizabeth groaned. "Sometimes I can't believe we're related."

Elizabeth loved her sister dearly, but at times Jessica was just too impossible. She thought of the time when they were really little and Jessica had talked her into climbing onto the roof of their house. Of course, Elizabeth was the one who slipped and nearly fell off.

Elizabeth knew she'd have to do something to keep Jessica away from Jeremy, or they would both end up losing their jobs. She didn't want that to happen. In the short time she'd worked at the hospital, she'd grown to love it.

What could she do to make Jessica stop hounding him? Threats wouldn't work—she knew her sister too well for that. Threatening Jessica was like waving a red flag in front of a bull. It only encouraged her.

Suddenly she had an idea. Maybe they could *scare* Jessica away. Of course, she would need Jeremy's help, but she was sure he'd be only too happy to cooperate. She thought about all the times Jessica had had a big crush on some guy, and then the minute he started paying attention to her, she began seeing all his flaws. If Jeremy made a big play for *her*, Jessica might cool off in a hurry.

The more Elizabeth considered it, the more

she liked the idea. She would talk to Jeremy about it as soon as she got off her break.

Jessica glanced at the clock. "Got to go," she chirped. "Miss North will have my hide if I'm late."

"I'm glad to see you're finally taking your job seriously," Elizabeth remarked coolly.

"I can't get fired now," Jessica said, "or I may never get the chance to make it up to Jeremy."

Elizabeth shook her head as her sister rushed off. The sooner she talked to Jeremy, the better. She got up, crumpled the cellophane wrapper from her cookie, and tossed it into the wastebasket.

Elizabeth was making her way down the corridor when she spotted Carl, the orderly, watching her from a doorway. A shiver rippled up her spine. Why was he staring at her like that? It gave her the creeps. The same thing had happened the week before, on her second day at the hospital. Several times she had had the feeling of being watched even when her back was turned. Once, she had whipped around quickly and had caught the flash of a white coat disappearing around a corner. She was almost certain it was Carl, but it made her nervous.

Even so, she made an attempt to be friendly. One of the nurses had told her that Carl was a real loner. He lived all by himself on the edge of town. As far as anyone knew, he didn't have a friend in the world. Elizabeth couldn't help feeling a little sorry for him.

She forced herself to smile at him. "Hi, Carl!" she said as she walked past the doorway.

Immediately he dropped his gaze and mumbled something that could have been "hello." His face had turned a dark, mottled red.

Elizabeth quickened her step. She had gone no more than a few yards past him when she could once again feel his gaze burning into her back. She fought the impulse to break into a run. *This is really silly*, she told herself. *Looks never killed anyone.*

What could he possibly do to her?

On Friday of that week Elizabeth was filing patient records for Mrs. Willoughby, the head nurse on Second Floor East, when Jessica came bursting into the office bearing an enormous bouquet of roses. Her cheeks were flushed with excitement.

"Look what Jeremy gave me!" she cried. "Wasn't that sweet of him? Somebody from the TV station sent them over, so he let me have them. Liz, I can't believe it! I think he actually likes me!"

"Maybe he's just allergic to roses," Elizabeth teased.

Jessica glared at her. "You're just jealous because he didn't give them to you."

"I'm absolutely green," Elizabeth said calmly.

"Don't try to deny it," Jessica went on, not even looking at her sister. "You know he likes me better. He even asked me today if I had a boyfriend."

"You're right, Jess. It must mean something. He never asked me that."

"I know you're going to say I'm imagining this whole thing," Jessica babbled on. "But I honestly do think he likes me."

Elizabeth smiled. "That's nice." She slid a rubber band around a batch of index cards.

"Oh, I know what you're thinking. You think he's too old for me. I'm only sixteen, and he's at least twenty-five. But everyone knows girls mature faster than boys. It's a fact."

"Absolutely."

Jessica frowned. "Of course, Mom and Dad won't see it that way. They'd probably forbid me to go out with him or something medieval like that."

"True love will find a way."

"So that's why I'm counting on you not to breathe a word of this to them."

"My lips are sealed."

Jessica stared at her. "You mean it? You really won't tell them?"

"Promise. Cross my heart." With an index finger Elizabeth traced an X across her chest.

"Elizabeth Wakefield, you're the best!" Jessica threw her arms around her sister, roses and all.

"Ouch!" Elizabeth cried as she was stuck by a thorn. But Jessica was already rushing out the door. She couldn't wait to call her friends and tell them the big news.

Nine

Later that day Elizabeth stopped at Jeremy's room. He was reading a magazine when she walked in. Looking up, he broke into a wide grin.

"Hi, Liz. How's it going? What's the latest with your sister? Any news on which way the hurricane is blowing?"

They had agreed upon using "hurricane" as the watchword for their conspiracy against Jessica.

Elizabeth giggled. "I think the winds are favorable. She went crazy over the flowers you gave her."

"Never let it be said I don't know how to win

the heart of a fair lady," he joked. "Besides"—he gave a mock grimace—"it's purely self-defense on my part. I know your sister means well, but if she doesn't stop showering me with attention, I may never get better!"

"I know what you mean. Jessica has a tendency to, uh—overdo things sometimes."

Jeremy chuckled. "I'm an old ham myself, so I know what it's like. I didn't get on TV by accident."

Elizabeth glanced at her watch. "Well, I guess I'd better get going. There's a new patient in two-twenty-seven. The nurse says she's a girl my age. I thought it might help if we talked. I know how lonely it can get being in the hospital."

"You're an angel!" Jeremy called to her as she was leaving.

"I just hope Jessica doesn't find out about any of this," Elizabeth responded, "or I may end up getting my halo bashed in!"

On her way down the corridor, Elizabeth spotted Carl, the orderly. She hurried past him, unable to shake the uneasy feeling that he was watching her out of the corner of his eye. She didn't think she was imagining it, but she hadn't mentioned it to anyone yet, not even Todd. What was there to tell? A person couldn't get arrested just for looking at someone.

Elizabeth forgot about Carl, though, the instant she walked into Room 227. She froze in her tracks, staring at the girl in the bed.

The new patient was Tricia Martin!

Elizabeth could hardly believe her eyes. Tricia looked so pale and fragile under the fluorescent lights that Elizabeth could see the faint violet tracing of veins at her temples. She lay very still, her chest barely moving as she breathed. An IV was taped to her arm. Suddenly Tricia's eyes fluttered open.

"Oh!" she gasped.

In a flash Elizabeth understood everything. Tricia never had a sick friend. She herself was the mysterious sick "friend" they had talked about. Elizabeth wondered why she hadn't realized it before. Undisguised by the loose dresses and thick sweaters she had worn at school, Tricia's slight frame looked gaunt and bony under the thin hospital shift. Against the backdrop of white linen, she was as pale as death.

Abandoning her cart, Elizabeth rushed over to her bedside. She seized Tricia's hand—it was so cold! "Oh, Tricia, why didn't you tell me you were sick? What's wrong with you?"

In a ragged whisper, Tricia replied, "I have leukemia, Liz."

Tears filled Tricia's eyes, but she was struggling not to give in to them. She kept her lips tightly clamped together and swallowed hard several times. A single tear escaped to trickle down her cheek.

"H-how bad?" Elizabeth managed to stammer past the rising lump in her own throat.

"I'm—I'm not going to get better."

"Tricia, no!" Elizabeth cried in shocked disbelief.

But looking at Tricia, she knew it was true. There was an expression of hopelessness in her eyes that couldn't be denied. Elizabeth could no longer hold back her own tears. They streamed down her face as she hugged Tricia. "Why didn't you tell us?"

Tricia tensed, her expression tightening. She shot Elizabeth a look of agonized determination. "I don't want Steve to know."

"But you can't keep it a secret!"

"Oh, he'll find out in a few months. But by then it won't matter so much. He won't be in love with me anymore. Don't you see? It's better this way." She gave a deep, shuddery sigh of resignation.

Elizabeth shook her head slowly. "You're wrong, Tricia. Steve would want to know."

Softly, but with that same fierce determination, Tricia repeated, "It's better this way." She said it in a manner that sounded as if she'd spent a lot of time trying to convince herself of it.

"You can't do this," Elizabeth pleaded. "Steve wouldn't want you to go through this alone. He loves you. He's miserable without you!"

"He'd be even more miserable if he knew the truth."

"But that's different! At least you'd have each other."

Tricia smiled wistfully. "For a little while."

"Isn't that better than nothing?"

"For me, yes," she said. "Not for Steve. He's the one who'll be left behind to pick up the pieces. No, Liz. I can't do it to him. I love him too much for that."

Elizabeth was overwhelmed with admiration for Tricia. Yet at the same time, she knew without a doubt that what Tricia was doing was wrong. Horribly wrong. Her decision would hurt Steven even more than if he knew the truth. Elizabeth was certain of it.

Tricia clutched at Elizabeth's hand. "Promise me you won't tell anyone—especially not Steve." Her eyes blazed from the shadowed hollows of her face. "Promise me, Liz!"

Elizabeth dropped her gaze. She stared down at the scuffed linoleum floor. "I promise," she said miserably.

"I knew I could trust you." Tricia beamed as she wiped the tears from her cheeks with a corner of the sheet. "In a funny way, I'm glad you know. Someday maybe you can tell Steve—a long time after I'm gone—that I really did love him. But then it won't matter so much. It's just that . . . I'd like him to know. Will you do that for me?"

Elizabeth was too choked up to speak, so she simply nodded. There was so much she wanted to say. She wanted to tell Tricia how sorry she was—and how glad she was to know her. But she couldn't seem to get the words to come out of her mouth.

Tricia seemed to have read her mind. "Please don't feel sorry for me," she said. "It was terrible when I first found out. I didn't want to believe what the doctors were telling me. But it's not so bad anymore. I've accepted it. It's strange, but whenever I used to think about dying, it really scared me. I thought it was the worst thing that could ever happen to anybody."

"And it isn't?" asked Elizabeth.

"No," Tricia said with a sad little shake of her head. "Living without love is worse than dying."

Elizabeth dabbed at her eyes with a balled-up tissue she'd fished from the pocket of her uniform.

"What about your family?" she asked. "How are they taking it?"

Tricia shrugged resignedly. "I don't think they've really accepted it yet. They're still talking about cures. Deep down they know, but it's a hard thing to admit. Yesterday I caught Papa looking through an old album of my mother's pictures. I could tell he'd been crying. I felt terrible. He depends on me so much. I worry about how he'll get along without me."

"It won't be easy for Steven either," Elizabeth reminded her gently.

A look of pain crossed Tricia's face. "He'll get over it. You'll see. It'll be easier for him this way. Just remember your promise, Liz. I'm counting on you."

"I—" She opened her mouth to tell Tricia that she didn't see how she could ever keep such a terrible promise, but she couldn't say no to the look of pleading on Tricia's face.

At that moment, one of the nurses walked in.

Tricia pressed Elizabeth's hand one last time. "Goodbye, Liz. And thanks for caring."

For the first time in her life Elizabeth realized how final the word goodbye could sound.

Ten

Elizabeth drove home in a stupor, hardly aware of Jessica's chatter beside her. She was too wrapped up in her thoughts about Tricia. If only there were some way of convincing Tricia what a terrible mistake she was making by not telling Steven! But she seemed so sure that what she was doing was right, even though it was obviously causing her tremendous pain. Elizabeth wished she could confide in her brother, but that was impossible, too. A promise was a promise, no matter how much she regretted making it.

"Elizabeth Wakefield, you haven't heard a

single word I've said!" Jessica's scolding tone broke through her dazed thoughts.

"Huh?" Elizabeth glanced over at her sister. "Sorry, Jess. I guess I had my mind on other stuff."

"What could be more important than this?" Jessica demanded petulantly. "The biggest celebrity in Sweet Valley is actually interested in me! Isn't that just the most fantastic thing you've ever heard?"

Elizabeth had forgotten all about Jeremy Frank. "Oh, that. Sure. I'm really happy for you."

"You don't sound as if you are. What's with you anyway? Ever since we left the hospital you've been acting like you're hypnotized or something. What gives?"

"Nothing," Elizabeth lied. There was no use dragging Jessica into this. Besides, Jessica was never any good at keeping secrets.

"You're not still mad at me because I fixed Steve up with Cara, are you?" Jessica asked.

Elizabeth sighed. "I just think you should have stayed out of it, that's all."

"It was for Steve's own good," Jessica insisted. "He was too stubborn to make a move, so I just gave him a little nudge."

"More like a big shove," Elizabeth said.

"Well, it worked, didn't it? He's forgotten all about Tricia now that he's got Cara."

Elizabeth frowned as she turned into their driveway. A tiny worm of fear uncurled inside her stomach. Could Jessica be right? Was Steven really getting interested in Cara? It didn't seem possible, but then Steven had been terribly hurt. He was an easy mark for a rebound relationship. All she could do was pray that Jessica was wrong.

The next week was misery for Elizabeth. In school she could hardly concentrate on what the teachers were saying. Homework was a total washout. Whenever she opened a book, all she could see was Tricia's sad, brave face. She kept hearing her voice: *"Promise me you won't tell Steve."*

But that promise was tearing her apart. How could she just stand by and do nothing while two people she cared about were suffering? Every instinct told Elizabeth that Tricia and Steven's breakup was wrong, yet she hated the idea of going back on a promise. It was Tricia's decision, after all. Did she have the right to interfere?

Making matters worse was the rumor that had been going around that Tricia had a new boyfriend. Elizabeth knew it wasn't true, but apparently there were a lot of people who believed it. On Friday Elizabeth was on her way to her locker between classes when she was accosted by Caroline Pearce, one of the biggest gossips in school.

"I saw you talking to Tricia Martin out on the

lawn last week," she said, her sharp eyes a contrast to the preppy primness of her neat red hair and plaid shirtwaist. "Did she say anything about her new boyfriend?"

"I don't know what you're talking about," Elizabeth muttered, trying to brush past her. But Caroline hung doggedly beside her.

"She probably just didn't want to tell you because of Steven. Lila said he looked older, so maybe he's a friend of Steven's. Hey, wouldn't that be something!"

Elizabeth turned to give Caroline a cold look. "It's all a bunch of dumb gossip," she said.

"Blame it on Lila," Caroline said with a shrug. "She's the one who started it. She said she saw them together."

"I don't believe it."

Caroline sniffed haughtily. "I don't see why not. Tricia's a Martin, after all. I wouldn't put anything past a Martin—including going out with her boyfriend's friend behind his back."

This was too much for Elizabeth. Bristling, she confronted Caroline. "For someone who talks a lot, you don't know very much!" she snapped, leaving Caroline to gape after her in openmouthed astonishment as she stalked off.

Despite her burning cheeks and the tears that stung her eyes, Elizabeth felt good to have finally told Caroline off after all the times she'd had to listen to her snobbish remarks. The trouble was, Caroline wasn't the only one who was prejudiced against Tricia because of her family. Look at the way Jessica felt. It was so unfair! Elizabeth thought. If only they knew what Tricia was really like, how sweet and wonderful she was. If they knew about the sacrifice she was making, they'd be ashamed.

Elizabeth was digging into her locker when someone touched her elbow. It was Enid Rollins, her best friend, and at this moment a very welcome sight. Enid's cheeks were pink, as if she'd been running. Her large green eyes sparkled with excitement.

"Guess what? I did it—I got an A on my chemistry quiz! I was so afraid I wouldn't make it. You know how tough Mr. Russo can be, treating us all as if we're budding scientists and—" Enid stopped to look at Elizabeth. "Liz, what's the matter? You look like you're about to cry. Did you and Todd have a fight?" she asked quietly, remembering the last time Elizabeth had looked this upset—the time she and Todd had almost broken up.

Elizabeth shook her head mournfully. "I wish that was all it was."

"Come on, we have a few minutes before our next class." Gently Enid steered her friend over to one of the benches that lined the corridor. "Do you want to tell me about it?"

Elizabeth moaned. "I can't. It's a secret, and I promised I wouldn't tell."

Enid was far too discreet to pry. She only nodded in sympathy. She knew what it was like to have secrets. And that was what friendship was all about—understanding and trusting, even when you didn't know all the facts.

"Are you sorry you promised? Is that what's bothering you?" Enid asked as if she'd read Elizabeth's mind.

Elizabeth buried her face in her hands. "Oh, Enid, it's all wrong! Everything. I never should have promised. How can a secret be any good if it's destroying the people it's supposed to be helping?"

"Some secrets shouldn't be kept," Enid replied. "Remember how afraid I was when I was going out with Ronnie? I was so afraid he'd find out about the trouble I'd gotten into when I was younger. It turned out to be a good thing when he found out. It showed me what a narrow person he was."

"This is different," Elizabeth said. "It's not really my secret, so I can't make that decision. I wish I could. I feel so awful about it, I don't know if I can stand it!"

"It sounds like too much responsibility for one person," Enid advised thoughtfully. "I think you need to talk to someone. Someone older. Can you tell your parents?"

"No. They're too close. Oh, Enid, how can I tell anyone? I promised!"

Enid slipped an arm around Elizabeth's trembling shoulders. "I can see what this is doing to you. Liz, you've *got* to tell somebody."

Elizabeth sensed that Enid was right, but she still remained uncertain. *Who?* she wondered. *Who can I tell?*

Eleven

"This is good, Liz. It shows a lot of feeling and enthusiasm. I think we should run it."

Mr. Collins, faculty adviser for *The Oracle*, held up the typewritten pages Elizabeth had turned in a few days earlier. It was the first in a series of articles she'd planned to call "A Candy Striper's Journal." She'd been enthusiastic about it when she started it, but now she could only shrug dispiritedly in spite of Mr. Collins's praise.

"Thanks," she said. "I guess I was feeling pretty enthusiastic when I wrote it."

"But you're not feeling that way now?" He perched on the edge of her desk, his sky-blue eyes intent on hers. "You're not thinking of giving up volunteering at the hospital, are you?"

"No, I still love it." She couldn't meet his gaze. Could he tell that she'd been crying? "It's just that—well, sometimes it can get to you."

"I know. I feel the same way about teaching sometimes."

Mr. Collins smiled warmly. He was by far the handsomest teacher in school, but that wasn't what Elizabeth liked best about him. What mattered to her was that he was the easiest teacher to talk to. She'd gone to him more than once in difficult situations. He was always sympathetic, never judgmental. He led her toward discovering the wisest course of action rather than coming right out and telling her what to do.

Elizabeth could feel herself on the verge of tears again. "It's awful when someone is sick, really sick, and you know—"

"Hey, Mr. Collins," John Pfeifer interrupted, "you should check out these pictures of Monday's game. They really came out well!" John, sports editor of *The Oracle*, waved a batch of prints under Mr. Collins's nose.

"Be with you in a minute, John," he said. "Liz and I are going up to my office. Hold the fort until we get back, will you?" To Elizabeth he said, "There's something I want to talk to you about. It's probably better if we do it in private."

Elizabeth nodded glumly, following Mr. Collins to the door.

"Take your time, Mr. Collins! I've got everything under control!" John called out, darting off in the direction of the light board. He nearly collided with Olivia Davidson, who was carrying a huge cardboard layout advertising an evening of one-act plays sponsored by the drama club.

Mr. Collins removed a stack of papers from the seat of a chair in his cluttered office. He motioned for Elizabeth to sit.

"I know how busy you are, Liz," he began, "but I have a favor to ask. It's about Max Dellon. I'm afraid he's not going to pass the next English test without some help."

Elizabeth tried to put Tricia out of her mind and focus on what Mr. Collins was saying. Max Dellon was the lead guitarist for The Droids, Sweet Valley High's resident rock band. Elizabeth knew that under Max's tough-talking, arrogant image there was a serious, talented musician. He was a little mixed up, but basically a nice guy.

"You're my best student," Mr. Collins went on. "I was hoping you could tutor Max. I've spoken with his parents about it, and they're willing to pay you for your time."

"Sure, Mr. Collins, I'd be glad to help," Elizabeth replied listlessly, her mind already drifting back to the conversation with Tricia.

"You don't seem very enthusiastic about it. Would you rather take a couple of days to think it over?" he asked kindly.

"No, that's OK. I—I guess I'm just not too enthusiastic about anything right now."

"So I see," he noted, adding gently, "Do you want to tell me what's bothering you, Liz?"

Elizabeth nodded, pressing her lips together to keep from crying. It was all right, she told herself. She could tell Mr. Collins. He would understand. He would help her decide what to do.

Suddenly the whole story came tumbling out— Steven and Tricia's breakup, finding out about Tricia's illness, the awful promise she'd made to the dying girl. Mr. Collins just listened quietly until she'd finished. Then he sighed deeply, folding his hands in front of him on the desk.

"I see your dilemma," he said.

"How can I break my promise to Tricia?" Elizabeth asked, twisting her hands in her lap. "It's her decision whether or not to tell Steve."

"That's true," Mr. Collins agreed. "But it's an unwise decision, I think. I know she's only trying to protect Steven, but she may end up hurting him even more this way."

"That's exactly how I feel."

"Have you tried talking to her about it?"

"I tried, but she's made up her mind. She's convinced it's the best way, even though I know she can't bear it. She really loves my brother, Mr. Collins. More than I ever realized."

"I'm sure she does, but Tricia's love is blinding her to the truth. She can't protect him from something like this. No one can."

"That's what I told her, but she wouldn't listen." In a burst of passion, she cried out, "It's not fair! Why did this have to happen? Tricia is one of the sweetest people I've ever known."

"Life can be very unfair sometimes," Mr. Collins agreed sadly.

Elizabeth was crying now, unable to control herself. "What am I going to do, Mr. Collins?" she said between sobs. "How can I break my promise to Tricia? She told me she's counting on me to keep this a secret." She put her head on Mr. Collins's desk and let loose a torrent of tears.

"Keeping your word is a good thing most of the time," he said, putting a comforting hand on her shoulder. "But every so often we make a bad promise. Then it's not right to keep it."

Elizabeth lifted her face to Mr. Collins. "How can I be sure it's a bad promise? How do I know I wouldn't be making a bigger mistake by telling Steve?"

"What do your instincts tell you?" he asked softly.

Elizabeth thought about it for a moment. Finally she said in a subdued voice, "I'm not sure why, but somehow I know what Tricia is doing is wrong. I think—no, I'm *sure* Steve would want to help her through this—this—" Her voice broke on a sob.

"Trust your instincts," Mr. Collins advised. "You have a good heart, Liz. Don't be afraid to follow it."

Elizabeth's sobs quieted, and she wiped her eyes dry. Then she looked up at her teacher and smiled thinly. "I think I know what I have to do now. Thanks, Mr. Collins."

It was painful. Decisions involving people's feelings were never easy. But it had to be done. She had to tell Steven.

Elizabeth was still sad when she left Mr. Collins's office, but she felt stronger and more sure of herself than she had in days. She only hoped she wasn't too late. Steven's date with Cara was that night. She wanted to talk to him before then, but she had to work at the hospital after school that day and might not get home in time. Another date with Cara, another chance for her to strengthen her hold on Steven.

"You'll never guess what happened!" Jessica hissed to Elizabeth when they bumped into each other in the hospital corridor. "Jeremy told me to come and see him on my break. He wants to talk to me, and he says it's important. What do you think it could be?"

"Maybe he wants to offer you a million-dollar contract to be his co-host," Elizabeth suggested.

Jessica giggled. "Don't be silly." But the thought had crossed her mind as well. "He probably just wants to ask me out."

"I can just see the two of you at the disco," said Elizabeth. "You'll be pushing him around the dance floor in a wheelchair."

Jessica sniffed. "Just because you're jealous, that's no reason to make nasty jokes."

"Who says I'm jealous?"

"It's perfectly obvious from the way you've been acting lately. I'm surprised Todd hasn't noticed."

Elizabeth was about to protest, but then she smiled, remembering the plan. "You're right, Jess. I'm so jealous I can hardly stand it. You're so lucky."

Jessica grinned. "It's not luck," she declared loftily. "The secret of success with men is knowing how to outfox them at their own game. Jeremy never had a chance."

Jessica hurried off in the direction of Jeremy's room. Her heart was pounding in anticipation of their meeting. Finally it was about to happen. Jeremy was going to make his move. Before she knew it, he'd be inviting her to appear on his show.

"Jessica, I thought you'd never get here!" Jeremy greeted her seductively. From his throne of pillows, he cast her a look that melted her insides.

"I got here as fast as I could," she said breathlessly. "I didn't even stop to comb my hair. I must look awful." She ran a hand over her hair, which of course was perfect, every silky strand in place.

"Never mind, you look beautiful." Jeremy extended a muscular arm. "Give me your hand." Jessica floated over to his side as if hypnotized. Instantly her hand was engulfed by his. "Jessica, there's something I have to tell you. I can't keep it inside any longer. I know you're only sixteen—"

"Sixteen and a half," Jessica corrected, nearly faint with wonder that this was happening to her. "And I'm very mature for my age."

"I know," he said, "or else I wouldn't have asked you to come here."

This was it! The big moment! He was going to ask her out. He probably had it all planned for when he got out of the hospital.

"What did you want to see me about?" she breathed, fluttering her lashes at him.

His fingers tightened around hers. "Somehow I just can't seem to get you out of my mind. Even in my dreams I keep seeing your face."

Jessica's eyes misted over. "Yes?"

"You're the girl I've been waiting for all my life."

"I am?"

"Jessica, darling, will you marry me?"

It was as if *he'd* just spilled a pitcher of ice water over *her*. Abruptly Jessica was jolted back to reality. "You've got to be kidding!"

"I've never been more serious in my life."

Jessica yanked her hand free and started backing away. "But—but I'm only sixteen!"

"A very mature sixteen," he recalled her words. "Besides, why should age stand in the way of true love? Think of Romeo and Juliet."

Jessica was thoroughly panicked by now. "I can't get married!" she squeaked. "I haven't even finished high school!"

"I can wait."

"Besides," she blurted out, "I don't love you!"

He laughed. "Darling, you don't have to pretend any longer! Do you think I'm blind? All your little excuses to come up to my room. Do you think I didn't know what you were really after?"

Jessica continued backing away. She banged into a chair, bruising her ankle, but she hardly noticed. "I—I never meant for it to turn out like this!"

"It doesn't matter anymore," he murmured huskily. "All that counts is now. I know it's sudden, but love is like that sometimes. It can hit you like a hurricane. Say it, Jessica. Say you'll marry me, my darling."

Giving a tiny, frightened cry, Jessica turned and fled. Out in the corridor she smashed into a hospital cart, sending it skidding into a wall. She didn't bother waiting for the elevator. She dashed down the stairs so quickly, she nearly fell.

Jeremy was chuckling softly to himself when Elizabeth poked her head into his room a few minutes later. He didn't say a word—he just gave her a thumbs-up sign.

Twelve

"Where's Steve?" Elizabeth asked the minute she and Jessica got home.

Mrs. Wakefield looked up from the blueprint that was spread out before her on the coffee table. She smiled, hooking a stray strand of honey-blond hair behind one ear.

"I haven't seen him," she said. "How did it go at the hospital today?"

"Fine," Elizabeth said.

"No comment," said Jessica, and acting as if she were hypnotized, she drifted upstairs. She'd been in a kind of trance ever since they had left the hospital, only coming out of it long enough on the way home to tell Elizabeth the incredible news about Jeremy.

"What's the matter with your sister?" Mrs. Wakefield asked. "Did something happen at the hospital?"

"You could say that." Elizabeth confessed to her mother the trick she and Jeremy Frank had played on Jessica.

Her mother laughed, her eyes twinkling with amusement. "Poor Jess! Well, she's probably gotten a real lesson out of all this, though I'm not sure what the lesson is. Honestly, the things you girls come up with! One thing about having twins—it never gets boring!"

"With Jessica, life could never get boring," Elizabeth agreed.

She was hoping Steven would show up for dinner so she'd have a chance to talk with him alone, but he didn't arrive until the family was sitting down to eat. In part, Elizabeth was relieved. She certainly wasn't looking forward to telling him about Tricia. At the same time, she couldn't stand the thought of his not knowing—and being angry at Tricia.

"Where are you taking Cara tonight, Steve?" Jessica asked, as if she hadn't already been filled in on every tiny detail. She and Cara had been talking about little else all week.

"My dorm is having a party," he said. He tried to smile, but a look of sadness still haunted his dark eyes. Elizabeth noticed it and winced.

"Cara just loves parties," Jessica said. "I'm sure you two will have a fantastic time."

"I intend to," Steven said, his jaw set.

"Isn't Cara the *sweetest*?" she gushed. "Any guy would be lucky to get her. You'd better not let her out of your sight for long at that party, Steve. Somebody else might snatch her away. You wouldn't want to lose her."

"No, I wouldn't want to lose her," Steven repeated softly, that faraway look in his eyes again.

It was all Elizabeth could do to keep from leaping across the table and strangling her sister. Why didn't Jessica just shut up about Cara? Poor Steven didn't stand a chance. Elizabeth had to talk to him before it was too late. If only she could get a moment alone with him after dinner.

But the chance never came. Steven excused himself almost as soon as he finished eating. "I promised Cara I'd pick her up by seven-thirty," he said, snatching up his jacket as he headed for the door.

"Have fun, Steve!" Jessica chirped.

Elizabeth said nothing. She was fighting to keep from dissolving into tears. Was Steven going to lose himself in Cara's relentless campaign to win him over?

The noise of the party thundered in Steven's ears. Everywhere he looked people were laugh-

ing, having a good time. He felt as if he were set apart from it all, an invisible spectator. He tried hard to concentrate on what Cara was saying.

". . . and remember I told everyone at my party about my mom running into Mrs. Morrow? The Morrows are the one's who're moving into the Godfrey mansion. Anyway, their daughter, Regina, is having this big party next Saturday, to get to know some of the kids at school. She sent out invitations to our whole class, and she said we could bring dates. Of course, I immediately thought of you, Steve. If you're not busy . . ."

His mind drifted off again. That was the week-end he'd planned on taking Tricia to Secca Lake. The last time they'd been there, they had packed a picnic lunch and hiked up the stream that fed into the lake. There was a place they discovered, a rock pool shaded by ferns and sweet-smelling pine trees, where they could swim in private. They spent the day dipping into the ice-cold water and basking in the warm sunlight. They talked quietly, planning their future together. Then they had kissed, and the kissing seemed to go on forever, sweet and delicate like Tricia herself. He remembered the feel of her bare arms against his back, the way her hair smelled of pine needles. . . .

"Steve, are you listening? Did you hear what

I just said?" Cara's strident voice broke into his thoughts.

"Huh? Oh, sure, Cara, I was listening," he lied.

"Do you want to go to Regina Morrow's party or not?"

"I—I don't know, Cara. I'll have to check my schedule. I have an awful lot of studying to do. Can I let you know in a couple of days?"

Cara pursed her glossy lips in disappointment. It was obvious she'd expected a more enthusiastic response. "Sure, I guess so."

Ted Foster, a boy Steven knew slightly, jostled his way toward them holding paper cups of punch, which he handed to Steve and Cara. "Hey, Steve! Long time no see. How's it going?" He gave Cara a long once-over, smiling in appreciation. "Say, is this the girl you were bragging to me about? Wow, I can see why! No wonder you keep her so well hidden."

Cara giggled and stuck out her hand, her cheeks flushed with pleasure at the unexpected compliment. "Hi," she said.

"Nice to meet you," Ted replied, shaking her hand. "Tricia, right? I never forget a name."

Cara flushed. "It's Cara."

Now it was Ted's turn to be embarrassed. "Uh, sure . . . Cara. Right. I got mixed up. Well, nice to meet you, Cara," he amended before slipping off into the crowd.

"Want to dance?" Steven asked in an attempt to smooth over the awkwardness of the moment.

Cara brightened. Putting down her punch, she snaked her arms around his neck. Swaying her hips gently as she moved to the rhythm of the music, she pressed in close against Steven. He could smell her perfume. Not like Tricia, he thought. She didn't have to wear perfume. The scent of her skin and hair was naturally delicate and sweet.

Steven screwed his eyes shut, willing himself to stop thinking about her. *Forget her! She's forgotten you by now. She has someone else.*

But he couldn't stop thinking about Tricia no matter how hard he tried. She kept drifting into his thoughts. He couldn't even force himself to be angry at her anymore. All he could remember was her sweetness, her lovely face, her sparkling laughter. Once, on his way to class, he'd seen a girl who looked a little like Tricia from behind, and he'd followed her halfway across the campus before he realized what he was doing.

"You seem a million miles away." Cara twisted her head to look up at him, her hair tickling him under the chin. She gave him a coy smile. "What's the matter? Don't you like being with me?"

"Sure I do," he said, swallowing hard against the lump in his throat.

"I'm glad to hear it. I mean, sometimes you

seem so far away, like you're not even with me."

"I guess I have a lot on my mind," he said.

Her pretty face puckered in a pout. "You're not thinking about Tricia, I hope!"

"No," he lied. "But since you brought it up, how is she?"

"You didn't hear? No one's seen her in about a week. My guess is that she dropped out."

Steven felt that familiar tightening in his chest again. "I can't believe that. She'd never drop out of school." Education meant so much to Tricia. She was determined to go to college, and since winning a scholarship looked like the only way she'd ever get there, she studied harder than anyone he knew. Once again he had the feeling that something was terribly wrong, something Tricia hadn't told him.

"The trouble with you is you're too nice, Steve," Cara scolded. "You never want to think the worst about anyone. Jessica says so all the time. But if you're going to be with me from now on, I don't want you thinking about *her*. After all, if we're going to be a couple—"

Steven stopped dancing. "Wait a minute," he said. "What's this about us being a couple?"

"Well, I figured since you and Tricia weren't going together anymore. . . ." Cara let her sentence trail off suggestively.

Steven broke away from Cara with an angry look. "Did you think I could replace Tricia just

110

like that?" he demanded. "As if she were a car or something? I loved Tricia!" He was aware of his voice growing louder, rising above the din of the music, but he didn't care what anyone thought. "If you want the truth, I still love her!"

Cara's eyes narrowed. "Forget it then," she hissed. "Let's just forget the whole thing. I was just kidding anyway. You didn't think I was serious, did you? I wouldn't be your girlfriend if you begged me!"

"Don't worry, Cara—I won't. Now why don't you get your things and I'll drive you home."

A grim smile touched Steven's lips as he strode out of the party, Cara trailing angrily at his heels. In a funny way he felt better than he had in weeks. He wasn't going to deny the way he felt about Tricia any longer. Maybe he wouldn't get her back, but that wasn't going to stop him from loving her.

Thirteen

Mrs. Jeremy Frank, Jessica doodled in her notebook. She smiled to herself. The more she turned it over in her mind, the better it sounded. The panic she'd felt in the beginning had worn off. She was starting to see the possible advantages to the situation she was in.

Of course there was no way she could actually marry Jeremy—not for a long time anyway. But an engagement? Why not? The idea had definite appeal. Imagine how impressed her friends would be when she showed off her diamond ring. Later on, if she changed her mind, she could always break it off. Meanwhile, she would reap all the benefits of being engaged to a celebrity. She might even become a celebrity herself. If they were engaged, Jeremy would have to put her on the show. Why hadn't she considered that before running out of his room today like some kind of idiot?

Well, it wasn't too late, she told herself. She would just go back and tell Jeremy she'd changed her mind. Humming something that sounded vaguely like "The Wedding March," Jessica wandered into her sister's room and plopped down on the bed.

"I've decided to accept," she said.

Elizabeth looked up from the article she was working on. "Accept what?"

"Jeremy's proposal. What else?"

Elizabeth's pen clattered to the floor. "Jess, what are you talking about? You can't marry Jeremy!"

"I didn't say I was going to marry him. I only said I was going to accept his proposal."

"But that's crazy! Jess, I won't let you do it." Elizabeth was panicking.

"I don't see how you can stop me," Jessica replied. Then she smiled dreamily. "Oh, Liz, think how much fun it'll be! Me, engaged to a big celebrity. Everybody will be positively green!"

"It's impossible," Elizabeth insisted. "Mom and Dad would never allow it."

"They wouldn't have to know. It could be a secret. I'll wear the ring around my neck so I can hide it inside my shirt whenever they're around."

"Jessica Wakefield, this is really the all-time dumbest idea you've ever had—and you've come up with some pretty dumb ones!"

Jessica's eyes narrowed to emerald slits. "You're just jealous because he didn't ask *you* to marry him." She leaped up off the bed. "I'm going over to the hospital now to tell Jeremy the good news."

Elizabeth was after her like a shot, grabbing her sister by the shoulders. "Wait! You don't know what you're doing! Jeremy's uh, . . . not what you think. He—" She gulped. "Well, I'll bet there's a lot you don't know about him."

"Who cares?" Jessica replied airily. "He's a celebrity. That's all that matters. Besides, we won't be strangers for long." Ignoring the protests Elizabeth continued to shout after her, Jessica dashed downstairs to see if she could talk her father into letting her borrow the car.

Mr. Wakefield was driving over to the office to pick up some papers he'd left there, so he said he'd drop her off, promising to pick her up on the way back. She gave him the excuse that she'd left one of her schoolbooks in the nurses' lounge.

"Thanks, Dad." She planted a kiss on his cheek as he dropped her off in front of the hospital.

114

"Anything for the cause," he answered with a wink.

If only he knew what a good cause it is, Jessica thought.

"Jessica?" The newspaper Jeremy had been reading fluttered to the floor. "What are you doing here this late? I wasn't expecting to see you again."

She flung herself across his bed. "Jeremy, can you ever forgive me for acting so silly this afternoon? I don't know what came over me. It was just the shock, I guess. But I thought it over—and I've decided to marry you after all."

For a full minute Jeremy simply stared at her without speaking. Then he burst into laughter. He laughed so hard his shoulders shook and tears streamed down his cheeks.

"What's so funny?" Jessica demanded.

When he could get the words out, Jeremy confessed the whole story, omitting only Elizabeth's part in it. "I'm sorry, Jessica. I suppose it was mean of me. It's just that you were so—enthusiastic," he said kindly. "I was only trying to cool you off a bit. I never thought it would backfire like this."

Jessica could feel her cheeks flaming with indignation. "You mean this whole thing was a joke? You never wanted to marry me—not even a little bit?"

"If I'd met you ten years from now, there'd be no doubt in my mind," he offered gallantly. "But sixteen *is* a bit young for marriage. You said so yourself."

"Well . . ." Jessica could feel herself relenting. In a strange way she was even a little relieved. Despite the assurances she'd given Elizabeth, she'd had her doubts about going through with it. Besides, she was already thinking of a way she could turn the situation to her advantage. "I guess you're right. I should at least finish high school before I start thinking about getting married. But that doesn't change the fact that you played a pretty dirty trick on me."

"I'd like to make it up to you," Jeremy said apologetically.

She sniffled, dabbing at her dry eyes with a corner of the sheet. "Maybe there is a way."

"Anything," he said.

"Anything?" Jessica grinned, her misery forgotten.

Elizabeth heard the slow, heavy tread of Steven's footsteps on the stairs. Then there was the sound of his bedroom door closing. What was he doing home so early? She walked down the hallway and knocked softly at his door.

"Come in," Steven's muffled voice replied.

She found him sprawled on the bed in his darkened bedroom, his face cradled in his arms.

116

"Steve." Elizabeth touched his shoulder. "What happened with Cara? Why did you come home so early?"

He gave a dry, bitter laugh. "I told Cara she was wasting her time. There's no use denying it anymore. I can't stop thinking about Tricia. I can't stop wondering who she's with. God, I love her so much!"

"She loves you, too," said Elizabeth gently.

Steven sat up. "That's a laugh. She couldn't care less about me."

Elizabeth shook her head sadly. "You're wrong, Steve. You don't know how wrong. I've talked to Tricia. She explained everything to me. She—she only broke up with you to protect you." There was a lump the size of a golf ball in her throat. When she tried to swallow, it only seemed to get bigger.

"Protect me? From what?" Steven gripped Elizabeth's arm. "What's going on, Liz? What did Tricia tell you?"

With a choked cry, Elizabeth threw herself into her brother's arms. "She made me promise not to tell you, but I can't keep it a secret anymore!" Brokenly, she got the story out while Steven listened, his face growing whiter by the moment.

"I guess there's no easy way of telling you this. Tricia's—she's dying. Of leukemia. I only found out by accident. She was in the hospital

117

for treatment. I'm so sorry, Steve. I wish I didn't have to be the one to tell you!"

With a choked sob, he buried his face in his hands. "Oh, God. Tricia. This isn't happening. She *can't* be dying!" Tears streamed down Steven's cheeks.

"I wish it weren't true," Elizabeth said.

When Steven finally raised his head, his expression had changed to one of grim determination. He stood up and grabbed his jacket from the back of the chair. "I've got to see her. Where is she?"

Elizabeth told him that Tricia had been sent home from the hospital after her most recent treatment. "Tell her I'm sorry, will you? Tell her I had to do it. I just couldn't stand watching either of you suffer any longer."

Steven stopped to give her a fierce hug. He was trembling, his chest still shaking with pent-up sobs. Elizabeth hugged him back, fighting her own tears. She had never felt so sad in her whole life.

"You should have called first." Tricia held the front door open just a crack and glared at Steven. Even though her heart soared with happiness at the sight of him, she couldn't let him know. There was too much at stake. So she lied. "I have a late date tonight. He's picking me up any minute. You'd better go."

She tried to close the door, but Steven pushed his way inside. With a glance, he took in the dingy, threadbare living room. Empty bottles and overflowing ashtrays littered the tables. The stale smell of liquor and cigarettes hung in the air. Tricia had always kept the house so tidy in the past. Now that she was sick, she probably didn't have the strength. Steven's heart wrenched with pain.

"You don't have a date, Trish," he said softly.

"You think I'm making it up? Anyway, what right do you have barging in like this?"

Her cheeks were flushed with emotion, but the rest of her face was deathly pale. She was wearing a fluffy sweater in a soft shade of blue that matched her eyes. Even though she was dying, she looked beautiful.

Steven shook his head sadly, tears welling up in his eyes. "Trish, baby, I know."

Tricia began to tremble at his words. What little remaining strength she'd been clinging to suddenly left her. Her legs wouldn't support her anymore. Uttering a strangled cry, she collapsed against Steven.

Fourteen

They stood there for a time, clinging to each other, both of them struggling desperately to hold in the tidal wave of their emotions. Silent tears streamed down Tricia's face, dampening the front of Steven's shirt. He stroked her hair gently, thinking how good it was to touch her again, in spite of everything.

"Oh, Steve." Her voice emerged as a cracked whisper. "How—how did you—" Her throat closed, shutting off the words.

"Liz told me," he choked, tears leaking from the corners of his eyes. "Tricia, why didn't *you* tell me?"

"I didn't want you to see me this way, Steve.

I didn't want you to watch me die a little bit at a time. I—I remember how it was with my mother. It hurt so much. I wanted to save you from that kind of hurt."

"Nothing could hurt me more than losing your love," he said.

"Oh, Steve, I never stopped loving you. I only told you that so I could set you free."

"Don't you know?" He touched her cheek. "I could never be free of loving you, not even if I tried. You mean everything to me, Tricia."

Tricia felt oddly weightless. The medication she was taking made her drowsy, and she couldn't help thinking this was all a dream. Except that Steven's presence was so warm and real.

"I missed you," she said.

"Me, too."

"I heard you were going out with someone else," he said. "Cara told me all about how you were hanging all over some guy in the drugstore."

Tricia was puzzled for a moment, but then she remembered. "That was the day I went to pick up my prescription and I almost fainted. There was a man—he helped me out to my car and drove me home. I suppose it *must* have looked as if I were all over him, but if he hadn't been there, I would have fallen down."

Steve grimaced. "I hate to think of you going through so much alone. Oh, Trish, you should have told me! Thank God Liz had the guts to break her promise."

"She was supposed to keep it a secret."

"I'm glad she didn't. Aren't you?"

Tricia thought for a moment, then nodded slowly. "Yes, I guess I am. I suppose it's selfish of me, but I can't help wanting you to be with me."

"I'm here." He stroked her hair. "I'm not leaving you this time."

"But I'll be leaving you," she said with soft regret. "Soon, I think."

"We still have time. And we have each other. That's the most important thing. We have each other for whatever time is left. Trish, I love you. I'll never stop loving you." His voice caught. "Even—even when you're gone."

For the first time in weeks, Tricia didn't feel cold. She felt Steven's warmth filling her up. When he brushed his lips against hers in a gentle, lingering kiss, she nearly cried out with happiness.

"It's funny," she said, "but I don't feel so afraid anymore. I feel stronger, like I can face anything. Even death."

Steven held her tightly. They were both crying, tears of sadness mingled with tears of happiness.

"I love you," she murmured thickly against his shoulder.

"I could go on holding you like this forever," he whispered.

Forever, she thought. Maybe forever wasn't such a long time for them, but when you loved someone as much as she loved Steven, a day could be forever, even a moment.

Tricia smiled as she looked up at him. "I heard about you and Cara," she chided gently. "Steve, how could you?"

"She's not so bad." Steven smiled back at her, brushing a stray lock from her forehead. "From about a mile away."

They both laughed and embraced tightly, their faces wet with tears.

"I love you," she whispered once again. "Don't ever forget that."

Steven knew he wouldn't. Part of Tricia would stay with him for the rest of his life.

Fifteen

"Wait till you see me on TV!" Jessica crowed over the phone. "I was great! Even Jeremy said so."

Elizabeth smiled. "Well, at least no one could accuse you of being modest."

Jessica had telephoned the hospital to talk to her sister as soon as she had returned home from the taping session for her segment of "Frankly Speaking." The show wouldn't be televised for a few weeks, but in her own mind Jessica was already a celebrity.

Elizabeth was sorry she'd missed the taping, but she'd promised to fill in for one of the nurse's aides who was on vacation. Anyway, she'd be seeing Jessica in all her televised glory soon enough.

"Aren't you happy for me, Liz?" Jessica demanded. "After all, when I'm a big celebrity, you'll probably have people asking for your autograph, too." She giggled. "They'll think you're *me*."

"I can hardly wait," Elizabeth said. "Really, Jess, I *am* happy for you. You deserve it after all the trouble you went through to get Jeremy to notice you. Even though *he* should probably get the Purple Heart."

"Very funny," Jessica responded, but nothing could dampen her mood. She went on chattering about the taping for several more minutes before Elizabeth was able to get off the phone and back to work.

Elizabeth glanced at her watch. Four-thirty already. Tonight was the night of the big party Regina Morrow was throwing. The party wasn't until eight, but she had to work until six, and then she had a tutoring session with Max Dellon right afterward. On top of everything else, she was supposed to drive to the party with Jessica, who wanted to get there early and be the first one to introduce herself to Nicholas Morrow, Regina's brother. At this rate Elizabeth would be lucky if she had time to change out of her uniform!

*   *   *

It had rained that afternoon, and the sky was overcast when Elizabeth left the hospital. As she walked out to the parking lot, her thoughts turned to Steven and Tricia. She was happy about the way things had worked out with them. They were closer than ever now. They spent every free moment together, and Tricia had confided in Elizabeth just the day before that she felt stronger about their relationship than ever. With Steven's love she could face anything, she said—even death.

Though Elizabeth knew it would be hard for Steven when Tricia was gone, she knew also that she'd done the right thing in breaking her promise. This way the loss, when it came, would be easier for him to bear.

Elizabeth was so absorbed in her thoughts she didn't notice that someone was following her—a short, husky figure in a white orderly's coat. His rubber-soled shoes made no sound as he tailed several yards behind Elizabeth. Carefully he skirted the puddles, prepared to duck behind one of the parked cars if Elizabeth should turn.

She angled toward the little red Fiat, parked beside a gunmetal-gray Chevy van she hadn't seen before. She quickened her step, at the same time fumbling in her purse for her car keys. She heard a noise behind her, and a flicker of nervousness darted through her. Probably nothing, she told herself. Nevertheless, she cast a quick glance around, hoping to be reassured by the sight of other people—a nurse or doctor getting off the latest shift, a family on their way in to visit a sick relative. But the parking lot was deserted.

It had grown chilly. The wind was blowing, rushing noisily through the leaves of the laurel trees that bordered the lot. Elizabeth wrapped her scarf about her neck and reached for the handle of her car door.

She slipped in behind the wheel and was turning the key in the ignition when she heard someone tapping on the window. Startled, she looked up. Dark eyes peered in at her. Her heart jumped into her throat.

Then she saw it was only Carl.

Elizabeth rolled the window down a crack. "Hi," she said, smiling to keep him from seeing how nervous she felt. "Did I forget something?"

"Uh . . . yeah." He spoke with effort, in a voice so husky it sounded as if he hardly ever used it. "Mrs. Willoughby wants to see you. She—she said it was important."

Elizabeth was confused. She'd spoken to Mrs. Willoughby just a few minutes earlier. Why hadn't she said something then? Well, it must have just come up. She shrugged and got out of the car.

That was when Carl leaped at her and clamped his hand over her mouth to stifle her scream. A fountain of terror rose in her. She struggled fiercely, torso twisting, legs flailing. But it was no use. Carl's grip was like iron, the pressure against her mouth unyielding. The only thing she managed to accomplish was to bite her own lip. Tears welled in her eyes as she tasted her own blood.

"I'm sorry, Elizabeth," Carl's gravelly voice whispered in her ear. "I promise I won't hurt you. I just want to be with you. The two of us. Forever."

Forever! What is he talking about?

Elizabeth gave a sharp yelp that was muffled by his hand. Bright dots of color swam before her eyes. Her struggles were growing weaker. He was too strong for her. She couldn't fight him.

The arm that was pinned across her chest slid away as Carl reached into his pocket for something. Before Elizabeth could lash out, a soft, wet cloth was jammed against her nostrils. A sickish-sweet smell enveloped her. Chloroform! She tried not to breathe in, but she couldn't help it. Waves of dizziness crashed over her. Her arms and legs felt very heavy.

A moment later Carl was dragging her toward the Chevy van. Through the haze that wrapped itself about her like layers of gauze, Elizabeth heard a click, then the back door opening. Carl lifted her sagging frame in his arms and placed her down gently on the mattress that was inside. He paused to smooth away a wisp of hair that was stuck to her cheek. Then the door slammed shut, and she could hear him walking around to the driver's door.

Got to get up . . . got to get away, Elizabeth thought, her brain still sending out feeble panic signals.

But she was so tired. Her head was spinning. Her arms and legs wouldn't budge when she tried to move them. When she opened her mouth to scream, only a tiny squeak emerged. It was like one of those nightmares where everything was in slow motion.

Where is he taking me? she wondered as the van's engine came to life.

Then everything went black. Elizabeth's last thought, as she slid into unconsciousness, was that this was no nightmare. This was real.

You'll have to wait an extra month to read the next book about Sweet Valley High, but it will be worth it!

Will Elizabeth be saved? Find out in Sweet Valley High #13, **KIDNAPPED.**

Announcing:

SWEET VALLEY HIGH
STAR-STUDDED
CONTEST

WIN!   WIN!   WIN!

***All-expense-paid trip to New York City
    for three

***A visit to the set of ABC-TV's
    ALL MY CHILDREN

***Tickets to a hit Broadway show

***A complete makeover at a top beauty salon

***Dinner with the creator of the series,
    Francine Pascal

<u>YOU</u> could be the lucky one to win all these fabu-
lous prizes! Contest entry instructions on next
page.

SWEET VALLEY HIGH STAR-STUDDED CONTEST

Here's How to Enter:

1 · Answer all questions in the Sweet Valley High Quiz. Write the letter of each correct answer in the space provided on the entry coupon located on the store display (or write your answers on a plain piece of paper). Please enter the *letter* of the correct answer only.

2 · Fill in your name and address in the space provided on the entry form and mail to:

SWEET VALLEY HIGH STAR-STUDDED
CONTEST
P.O. BOX 1035
SO. HOLLAND, IL 60473

3 · A separate contest in Canada provides for a Canadian winner. Residents of Canada send their quiz answers to:

SWEET VALLEY HIGH SOAP OPERA
CELEBRATION
P.O. BOX 8007
OSHAWA, ONTARIO L1H 8K7

4 · Entries must be postmarked no later than OCTOBER 31, 1984.

SWEET VALLEY HIGH QUIZ:

Test your knowledge of the happenings of Sweet Valley High! To enter the Star-Studded Contest, write the letter of each correct answer in the space provided on the entry coupon (or on plain paper). Fill in your name and address and send to the address listed on the coupon.

GOOD LUCK!!!

1. What did Elizabeth see Lila Fowler shoplift?
   - (a) Gold bracelet
   - (b) Silk scarf
   - (c) Earrings
   - (d) Gold chain

2. Who took Robin to the Discomarathon?
   - (a) Tom McKay
   - (b) Bruce Patman
   - (c) Allen Walters
   - (d) Winston Egbert

3. What is Jessica elected queen of?
   - (a) Homecoming
   - (b) Sweet Valley High
   - (c) Spring
   - (d) Fall

4. In whose locker does Jessica tell Robin to put the chemistry test answers?
   - (a) Emily Mayer
   - (b) Dana Larson
   - (c) Lila Fowler
   - (d) Enid Rollins

5. A rumor circulates around the school that Ms. Dalton is having an affair with one of the students. Who is he?
    (a) Allen Walters
    (b) Ken Matthews
    (c) Tom McKay
    (d) Scott Henderson

6. Whose father is a Hollywood agent?
    (a) Patsy Webber
    (b) Mandy Farmer
    (c) DeeDee Gordon
    (d) Suzanne Hanlon

7. Which of these girls was briefly a model?
    (a) Julie Porter
    (b) Annie Whitman
    (c) Cara Walker
    (d) Dana Larson

8. Lila Fowler gives a costume party. Elizabeth and Jessica dress as what?
    (a) Fifties' characters
    (b) Pirates
    (c) Gypsies
    (d) Matadors

9. What is Elizabeth's favorite sleepwear?
    (a) Nightshirt with UCLA on it
    (b) Large T-shirt belonging to Todd
    (c) Shirt belonging to her brother Steven
    (d) Nightshirt that Jessica gave to her because it was "unsexy"

10. What is Elizabeth's favorite drink?
    - (a) Ginger ale
    - (b) Vanilla milkshake
    - (c) Root beer
    - (d) Orange soda

11. Who of the following is *not* a member of Pi Beta Alpha?
    - (a) Caroline Pearce
    - (b) Elizabeth Wakefield
    - (c) Olivia Davidson
    - (d) Cara Walker

12. What is the name of the Sweet Valley High basketball team?
    - (a) The Gladiators
    - (b) The Hawks
    - (c) The Droids
    - (d) The Trojans

13. What is the name of the Fowler estate?
    - (a) Fowler Manor
    - (b) Fowler Crest
    - (c) Thornhurst
    - (d) Fowler Circle

14. What is the name of the ice cream parlor in the Sweet Valley mall?
    - (a) Kelly's Place
    - (b) Casey's Place
    - (c) The Dream Machine
    - (d) Fast 'n' Frosty

15. What physical feature distinguishes the Wakefield twins?
    (a) Elizabeth has a dimple, Jessica does not
    (b) Elizabeth is one inch shorter than Jessica
    (c) Elizabeth has a small mole on her right shoulder
    (d) Jessica has a small mole on her left shoulder

16. What color is Jessica's bedroom?
    (a) Sky blue
    (b) Maroon
    (c) Brown
    (d) Cream

17. Who of the following is the bass guitarist for The Droids?
    (a) Dan Scott
    (b) Dana Larson
    (c) Bill Chase
    (d) Guy Chesney

18. How much older is Elizabeth than Jessica?
    (a) Eight minutes
    (b) Four minutes
    (c) Three minutes
    (d) Ten minutes

19. What color was the motorcycle helmet that Todd bought for Elizabeth?
    (a) Silver
    (b) Hot pink
    (c) Fire-engine red
    (d) Yellow

20. Who is the manager of the cheerleading squad?
    (a) Ronnie Edwards
    (b) Susan Stewart
    (c) Sandra Bacon
    (d) Ricky Capaldo

21. With whom does Jessica get stuck in a boathouse?
    (a) Scott Daniels
    (b) Rick Andover
    (c) Aaron Dallas
    (d) Danny Stauffer

22. What is the "Lover's Lane" of Sweet Valley High?
    (a) Secca Lake Road
    (b) Miller's Pond
    (c) Palisades Way
    (d) Boulder Bluff

23. Roger Barrett has a big secret. What is it?
    (a) His mother is an alcoholic
    (b) He has a heart-throbbing crush on Cara Walker
    (c) He has a police record
    (d) He works part time as a janitor

24. What is Bruce Patman's favorite sport?
    (a) Surfing
    (b) Track
    (c) Tennis
    (d) Basketball

SWEET VALLEY HIGH
STAR-STUDDED
CONTEST

<u>Official Rules:</u>

1. Enter by sending answers to the Sweet Valley High Quiz in the back of Book #12 of the Sweet Valley High series on a completed entry form or plain piece of paper (with your name and address) to the following address if from the United States:

SWEET VALLEY HIGH STAR-STUDDED CONTEST
P.O. BOX 1035
SO. HOLLAND, IL 60473

Or, if from Canada, to:

SWEET VALLEY HIGH SOAP OPERA CELEBRATION
P.O. BOX 8007
OSHAWA, ONTARIO L1H 8K7

Enter as often as you wish. All entries must be handwritten (not mechanically reproduced). Each entry must be in a separate envelope bearing sufficient postage. No purchase necessary. *Entrants from Canada only must also add the universal product code number from any bottle of Noxema Antiseptic Skin Cleanser or package of Noxema Antiseptic Skin Cleanser Pads.*

2. One prize will be awarded to an entrant from the United States and one to an entrant from Canada. Each prize includes return economy air travel for three (3) from the commercial airport nearest the winner's home to New York City; two-night hotel accommodation (triple occupancy); and airport/hotel ground transfers. While in New York, the winner and two guests will be present at a rehearsal of ABC's *ALL MY CHILDREN*, receive a makeover at a beauty salon of Bantam's choice (winner only), see a Broadway show of Bantam's choice, and have dinner with the creator of the Sweet Valley High series, Francine Pascal. All other meals will be provided. No other

expenses are included. Each prize must be accepted as awarded (no cash substitutes), and travel must be completed by April 30, 1985. Minors must be accompanied by a parent or guardian. Approximate value of prize for entrants from Canada $1,600.00 (U.S.) (e.g., Toronto departure) or more depending on departure point (e.g., Vancouver, $4,000.00 [U.S.])

3. A random draw by country will be made from all entries postmarked no later than October 31, 1984, the contest closing date. To win, the selected entrants must have correctly answered the Sweet Valley High Quiz, and in the case of entrants from Canada, subsequently correctly answer a time-limited arithmetical-skill-testing question to be administered by telephone at a mutually convenient prearranged time. The chances of winning are dependent upon the number of entries received by country.

4. All entries are subject to verification for eligibility. All entries become the property of Bantam Books, Inc., and none will be returned.

5. Bantam Books, Inc. is not responsible for entries lost, misdirected, or delayed in the mail or otherwise.

6. By entering, entrants agree to the use, without charge, of their name, address, and photograph for publicity purposes.

7. This contest is offered only in the continental United States, Hawaii, Alaska, and Canada (except Quebec). Employees of Bantam Books, Inc. and ABC-TV or their subsidiaries and affiliates, and distributors, dealers, advertising and promotion agencies, or members of their immediate families are not eligible. Contest is void where prohibited by law and is subject to all federal, state, provincial, and local regulations.

8. The Sweet Valley High Quiz may be obtained by sending a self-addressed, stamped envelope to Bantam Books, SVH Quiz Request, Dept. TB, 666 Fifth Avenue, New York, NY 10103. In Canada, send quiz requests to Bantam Books Canada, Inc., SVH Quiz Request, 60 St. Clair Ave. East, Suite 601, Toronto, Ontario M4T 1N5.